JUMP SHOT

JUMP SHOT

Tiki Barber and Ronde Barber
With Paul Mantell

A Paula Wiseman Book
Simon & Schuster Books for Young Readers
New York   London   Toronto   Sydney   New Delhi

SIMON & SCHUSTER BOOKS FOR YOUNG READERS
An imprint of Simon & Schuster Children's Publishing Division
1230 Avenue of the Americas, New York, New York 10020
SIMON & SCHUSTER BOOKS FOR YOUNG READERS
is a trademark of Simon & Schuster, Inc.
For information about special discounts for bulk purchases,
please contact Simon & Schuster Special Sales at 1-866-506-1949
or business@simonandschuster.com.
The Simon & Schuster Speakers Bureau can bring authors
to your live event. For more information or to book an event,
contact the Simon & Schuster Speakers Bureau at 1-866-248-3049
or visit our website at www.simonspeakers.com.
Book design by Hilary Zarycky
The text for this book is set in Egyptienne
Manufactured in the United States of America • 1013 FFG
2 4 6 8 10 9 7 5 3 1
Library of Congress Cataloging-in-Publication Data
Barber, Tiki, 1975–
Jump shot / Tiki and Ronde Barber ; with Paul Mantell.
pages cm
ISBN 978-1-4424-5729-4 (hardcover : alk. paper)
ISBN 978-1-4424-5731-7 (eBook)
1. Barber, Tiki, 1975– —Childhood and youth—Juvenile fiction.
2. Barber, Ronde, 1975– —Childhood and youth—Juvenile fiction.
[1. Barber, Tiki, 1975– —Childhood and youth—Fiction. 2. Barber, Ronde,
1975– —Childhood and youth—Fiction. 3. Basketball—Fiction.
4. Teamwork (Sports)—Fiction. 5. Twins—Fiction. 6. Brothers—Fiction.
7. African Americans—Fiction.] I. Barber, Ronde, 1975– II. Mantell, Paul.
III. Title.
PZ7.B23328Ju 2013
[Fic]—dc23
2013000110

For AJ, Chason,
Riley, and Ella—T. B.

For my three roses—R. B.

Acknowledgments

The authors and publisher gratefully acknowledge Mark Lepselter for his help in creating this book.

JUMP SHOT

1

A NEW DOOR OPENS

"Thanks, man." Ronde Barber exchanged an elaborate handshake with one of his many fans at Hidden Valley Junior High School.

"Yeah, dude, thanks a lot," said Ronde's identical twin, Tiki, slapping the boy on the back.

"No, thank *you* guys. For *everything.*"

Ronde didn't even know the kid's name. He didn't know him, and he was pretty sure Tiki didn't either.

It happened a lot like that. These days, in the second term of their last year at Hidden Valley Junior High, the Barber twins were "Big Men on Campus"—stars of the school's history-making football team. The Eagles had been State Champions two years running and, this past season, owners of a perfect record.

Everyone knew their names all right, even at a big

school like Hidden Valley. But there were plenty of kids whose names Tiki and Ronde didn't know, or had forgotten.

It wasn't that they were stuck up about their superhero status. Not at all. But it was hard to remember everyone's name who knew yours, when yours had been plastered all over the school paper, the local TV news, the *Roanoke Reporter*, and even newspapers as far away as Richmond.

Remembering names wasn't a big problem by any means. It was great being popular. The only real problem was, their football career at Hidden Valley was *over*. Ever since the final celebrations had ended, Ronde's and Tiki's lives had become more and more . . . well, *boring*. Oh, school was okay, and it was fun catching up on their favorite TV shows—but it was *winter*, and it was *cold*, and there was nothing really important going on in their lives anymore!

No practices to get their blood pumping. No video strategy sessions with the team to get their minds racing. No big games to look forward to every week.

It was only the end of January, but to Ronde, it felt like winter had been dragging on for months! And here they were, on a Thursday afternoon that had already turned dark by four o'clock, waiting to get into the gym so they could sit in the bleachers, crammed in with all their friends and those other kids whose names they didn't even know or couldn't remember . . . just to *watch* a *basketball* game!

Watching was not the same as playing, Ronde thought sadly. And basketball, while it was fun, was only the Barbers' second-favorite sport. Besides, while Hidden Valley Junior High had always been a powerhouse in football, it had never done well in basketball. The team hadn't won a league championship in forty years, and for five straight seasons, they'd fallen short of making the play-offs.

This year's team was better than most, but their record was only about .500 at this point, midway through the season. And the only reason it wasn't worse was the team's all-star point guard, Sean Morton.

Sean was only in eighth grade, but he was already a league all-star, and was being talked about for the All-Virginia team. Sean—or "Sugar," as everyone called him for his sweet jump shot—was averaging twenty points a game, and his brilliant ball-handling was reason enough to come see an Eagles game.

So the bleachers were packed. And most of them were here not so much to root for the team, as to see "Sugar" put up some serious numbers.

"I can't believe this is the first game we've been to this year," Tiki said as they climbed up into the bleachers and found two seats together, way back near the top row.

"I know," Ronde said, sitting down. "It's weird being in the stands, watching the game."

"Tell me about it." Tiki reached into his coat pocket and pulled out a bag of peanuts. "Want some?"

Ronde cupped his palm and caught the peanuts just as the game began. Sugar, wearing number 1 on the back of his uniform, with EAGLES on the front in capital letters, caught the tip-off and dribbled upcourt. His ball-handling was impressive—fancy moves, a through-the-knees fake, then a no-look pass to the shooting guard, Brian Reynolds. Reynolds, with a clear look at the basket, put up a shot—and missed.

Sugar groaned out loud, shook his head, and made a face before retreating back upcourt.

Reynolds was slow getting back, and the player he was supposed to be guarding sank an easy running layup to start the scoring.

"Come on!" Sugar shouted, gesturing for Reynolds to kick it into gear.

Ronde looked at Tiki, who returned his gaze. Like many sets of identical twins, they often found that they were thinking the same thing at the same time. Right now was one of those times. Ronde knew Tiki was also thinking about Cody Hansen, their quarterback on the Eagles when they were in eighth grade.

Cody used to yell at his teammates like that. And it never worked, either.

Sure enough, these basketball Eagles soon found themselves trailing badly. And the more they fell behind, the more Sugar Morton held on to his dribble, taking most of the shots himself, and not including his teammates much. The rest of the Eagles seemed to be moving a step slower than Sugar. Slower than their opponents, the Colts of Martinsville Junior High, as well.

By halftime, Sugar had scored twenty-two points, but the rest of the Eagles had managed a paltry five. That made the score 36–27, Patriots. Thirty-six was a lot of points for one half, showing that the Eagles were barely bothering to play defense.

"Sure glad we're not in that locker room," Tiki said as they waited for the second half to start.

"Yeah. We were lucky. At least we were always in the hunt for a play-off spot," Ronde said.

"These guys'll never make it, the way they're going. They'll be lucky to finish over .500."

"Yeah, and they should be much better, with a guy like Sugar chuckin' it up there like that."

"Oh, well," Tiki said, shrugging. "Not much we can do about it from up here."

The second half began with Sugar on the bench, steaming about something. *Probably the way his teammates are playing*, thought Ronde.

When Sugar finally got back in the game, the Eagles

were trailing by fifteen points. He proceeded to put on a one-man show, sinking shot after shot, even though the Colts were constantly double-teaming him.

"He's got an open man!" Tiki shouted more than once. But Sugar never seemed to want to let go of the ball unless he was launching it toward the basket.

In the end, he made the score fairly close—67–63—but the Eagles still wound up on the short end of the stick.

Tiki and Ronde left the gym along with the rest of the crowd. They crossed the parking lot and kept walking, headed for the public bus stop a block farther down James Street. It wasn't the time of year to be riding bikes—too cold for that—and there were no school buses this late in the day.

Riding home, the brothers didn't say much at first. Each was absorbed in his own private thoughts. Finally, Tiki muttered, "Man, this really rots, you know?"

Ronde knew what he meant. "Not being part of the team anymore? Yeah. I know."

"Life's just not the same. It's like something's missing."

"Well, we've still got classes," Ronde said. "And you're gonna be writing your advice column for the school newspaper."

"Ugh, don't remind me," Tiki said, making a face. "I wish I'd never promised Laura I'd do that after the season ended." Laura Sommer was the editor and publisher of the *Hidden Valley Gazette*, which she had turned from a one-page handout to a real, twice-monthly newspaper that the whole school looked forward to reading.

"Point is, you promised her you'd do it," Ronde said. "And while you're at it, who knows, you might wind up helping somebody out there."

"Yeah, right," Tiki said, dismissing the thought.

But Ronde could tell he'd made his point. "Besides, there's also the job at Mr. Landzberg's warehouse," he said. "He offered us twenty hours a week, and said we could split the job between us if we wanted. That could end up being a lot of money."

Justin Landzberg had been a teammate of theirs on the Eagles, and his dad owned a local department store with its own warehouse. "They always need stockboys," Justin told them when they informed him that they were fourteen now, and able to get working papers.

Tiki and Ronde's mom worked two jobs. Times were tough in Roanoke, and it was hard for a single mom to make enough money to bring the boys up and pay all the bills. The twins had always wanted to help by contributing to the family budget, but until now, they'd been too young.

"I guess you're right," Tiki said, still thinking about their days of glory on the football field. "I mean, all things come to an end, right? Even the best things."

"It was the best, wasn't it?" Ronde remembered with a smile. "They can never take those championships away from us."

"Or that perfect season."

"Or all those great plays . . ."

"All the comebacks . . ."

They both sighed, and fell silent again.

"I'm never gonna forget it," Tiki finally said. "Even if we make it to the NFL."

Ronde gave him a playful shove. "What do you mean, 'if'?"

"Still," Tiki said as their stop approached. "I wish we had something fun to do between now and next fall."

"You never know," Ronde said as they got off the bus. "Something might turn up tomorrow morning."

Little did he know how right he was.

"Yo! Ronde!"

Ronde turned from his locker to see Mr. Jackson coming toward him. Mr. Jackson was his science teacher, and immediately Ronde thought he must have messed up on the latest quiz or homework assignment. But the smile on Mr. Jackson's face told a different story.

"What'd I do?" Ronde blurted out.

"Nothing! What are you worried about?" Mr. Jackson said with a chuckle. "Last I looked, you were running an A minus."

Ronde beamed. He was good at science, and proud of it too.

Mr. Jackson's smile faded. "Look, Ronde, you got a minute? I need to talk to you about something. Or you could come to my office fourth period. You have lunch fourth period, right?"

"We can talk now," Ronde said. "I've got study hall."

"Good, good," said Mr. Jackson. "Let's sit on that bench over there in the lobby. It'll quiet down soon as passing's over."

Two minutes later, the halls had emptied, and they could hear themselves think. "Here's the thing," Mr. Jackson began. "It's about the team, basically. I've got a problem I'm hoping you or your brother can help me with."

In his panic about his science grades, Ronde had forgotten that in addition to being his science teacher, Mr. Jackson was also Hidden Valley's basketball coach.

"The team is in trouble," Mr. Jackson said. "And now I come to find out that Brian Reynolds is transferring out; going to military school, starting Monday."

"Whoa. That's too bad," Ronde said. Brian was the team's starting shooting guard. He scored more points than anyone on the squad except Sugar. "But—"

"But how can you help? That's what I was about

to ask you!" Mr. Jackson's smile returned. "I can move Rory Mathis up to starter. But now I've got an opening on my bench, with no obvious candidates to fill it. So I'm asking myself, 'Who at this school might be good at basketball, but didn't try out for the team, for whatever reason. . . .'"

In the silence, Ronde realized what Mr. Jackson was offering. "You mean *us*?"

Mr. Jackson put both hands out, palms up. "I didn't call you aside just to chat."

Ronde swallowed hard. His heart was suddenly racing with excitement, but he tried not to show just how eager he was.

"You know, I'm sure we'd be interested, Mr. J. We're always playing one-on-one in the driveway, you know, and we can handle the ball pretty well. Although neither of us is a great *shooter*," he warned, not wanting the coach to get too hopeful. After all, Mr. Jackson was asking them to fill in for a *shooting* guard, wasn't he?

"Well, I understand why you both never came out for tryouts," Jackson said. "I know Coach Wheeler didn't want either of you getting hurt doing any other sports."

Ronde nodded. It was true. Football had always been the most important thing to him and Tiki. It was true that they often played hoops in their driveway, although not "always," as he'd told Mr. Jackson. They'd played some pick-up baseball too, in summer, and run races against each other for fun, just like any two athletic brothers on planet Earth.

But joining the basketball team was another step up, for sure. Why shouldn't they try their hand at other sports, now that they didn't have to worry about football until high school? In fact, Ronde made a mental note, right then and there, to try out for the baseball team in early March.

"Don't misunderstand me," Mr. Jackson said, holding up a hand. "I've only got *one* spot on the roster. I'll leave it up to you and Tiki which of you wants to give it a try."

Ronde froze, with his jaw wide open. He'd been about to say something else, but now, for the life of him, he couldn't remember what it was.

Only *one* of them was going to be on the basketball team?

WHICH ONE??

2

SIBLING RIVALRY

"You told him WHAT??" Tiki's eyes opened so wide it felt like his eyeballs were going to pop out. "I can *too* shoot!"

Ronde cocked his head to one side. "I don't know. . . ." he said.

"*What?* I can shoot rings around you, Ronde!"

"Cannot."

"Can too!"

"Nuh-uh."

"Come on, I'll show you." Tiki grabbed his brother by the shirt and started dragging him out to the driveway. "One-on-one. Come on, I'm gonna show you who can shoot and who can't."

Ronde resisted, digging his rubber-soled sneakers into the floorboards. Tiki managed to drag him a foot or two, but that was it.

"What, are you scared?" Tiki taunted him. "You know I can outshoot you any day."

"I didn't say you couldn't!" Ronde protested. "I only said neither one of us was a great shooter."

"Don't put me in the same boat with you," Tiki said angrily. "You shoot a basketball like it's a brick!"

"Okay," said Ronde, removing Tiki's hand from his shirt. "Now you've gone and done it. I'm no worse a shooter than you. Plus I play better defense."

"Okay, that's it," said Tiki. "Are you gonna play me one-on-one right now, or are you gonna chicken out?"

"*Chicken out?*" Ronde repeated, his own eyes opening wide. "*Me?*"

"Who said 'chicken'?" called their mom, who was just coming in the front door. "How did you know I was making chicken tonight? Are you psychic?"

She let out a hearty laugh and crossed the room, headed for the kitchen with her two heavy shopping bags in each hand and her purse slung over her shoulder.

It was Thursday, one of the few days of the week when Mrs. Barber had to go to only one of her jobs. She put in over sixty hours a week in total, so it was a treat for them all to have dinner as a family. Ronde and Tiki ran to take her heavy bags and help her carry them.

"Mom," said Tiki, "Mr. Landzberg says we can have twenty hours at his warehouse to split between us any way we want."

Mrs. Barber beamed. "That's wonderful!" she said, putting an arm around each of their shoulders. *We're almost as tall as she is now,* Tiki noticed. He saw her notice it too, and her eyes glistened with feeling. "My two big boys," she said. "I hope you'll like working for him. Are you sure your schoolwork won't suffer?"

"Don't worry, Mom," said Ronde. "We can handle it!"

"And not only that!" Tiki blurted out. "I'm gonna be on the basketball team!"

"You *what*?" Mrs. Barber said, taken aback.

"He's wrong, Ma," Ronde said. "*I'm* the one who's gonna be on the team. Tiki's too busy with his *advice column*." He shot Tiki a look, and Tiki shot it right back at him.

"What in the world is going on here?" she said, stopping them both from going at each other. "Which one of you is going to explain it to me?"

"I will!" they both said at once.

"One at a time," said their mom.

Tiki got his word in edgewise first. "There's only one spot on the team, so Ronde will take the job at the store."

"What about that advice column?" Mrs. Barber asked, looking straight at Tiki.

"I'll take care of it," Tiki said, his teeth clenched together. "I can handle whatever."

"I'm not so sure of that," Mrs. Barber said. "See that

you do—both of you. I don't want to see either of your grades go down, no matter what happens. That's more important to me—and to you—than any amount of money you make. Understand?"

They both nodded. *She's leaving it up to us to solve the problem,* Tiki understood.

"How much time till dinner's ready?" Ronde asked.

"Half an hour," she replied, and might have been about to say something else, but neither boy hung around long enough to find out what it was.

Ronde fished the ball out of the corner bin in the garage, while Tiki dug the pump out of a pile of sports equipment in the corner. "First one to eleven baskets wins," Ronde said as he flipped a coin. "Dang. Tails. You win."

Having won the toss, Tiki started out with the ball as they started a high-stakes game of one-on-one. He tried to fake his brother out, but three years of playing pass defense on the football team had made Ronde great at sticking with his man. No matter what Tiki tried, Ronde stuck to him like glue. Finally, in frustration, Tiki threw the ball up—and Ronde leaped high in the air to block it!

Tiki somehow managed to retrieve the ball before it went onto the front lawn and out of bounds. "Man, I'll say one thing—you sure can play defense," he told Ronde.

"Is that a complaint?" Ronde said, smiling.

This time, Tiki wasted no time in shooting. Before Ronde knew what was happening, the ball was in the air and—swish!—through the hoop. "One–nothing, mine!" he crowed.

"What'd I say?" Tiki taunted him. "*Who* can't shoot?"

"Zip it!" Ronde said, stealing the ball from him just as Tiki was grabbing the rebound. "Ha! Take that!"

Now it was Tiki's turn on defense. Unlike Ronde, he was not used to covering other people. In football, it was always the other team's job to defend *him*, not the other way around.

Now, with Ronde dribbling from one hand to the other, faking with his head and feet, Tiki was forced into guessing which way he was headed—and he guessed *wrong*. The result was an easy layup for his twin, tying the score, 1–1. "That's what I'm talkin' about!" Ronde bellowed.

Tiki touched the ball and handed it back to Ronde at the top of the key. This time Tiki told himself not to commit too quickly—to wait for Ronde to make his *real* move first.

That sounded good in theory, but in reality, it meant his twin got a full step on him, and was able to get to the hoop. Luckily for Tiki, Ronde missed the easy layup.

"Man!" Ronde groaned as Tiki retrieved the rebound. "I *told* you we couldn't shoot!"

"Speak for yourself," Tiki shot back, launching another quick shot that sailed right through the hoop.

Their net had fallen apart long ago, or Tiki's shot would have made that sweet *swish*ing sound.

Ronde tossed Tiki the ball back. This time, Tiki tried to dribble past Ronde on his left side. Ronde, fooled by the move, gave him a little shove. "Foul!" Tiki cried.

"What are you, the referee?" Ronde said. "That was a clean takeaway!"

"You pushed me!"

"Hey, it's a contact sport," Ronde offered.

"My ball," Tiki insisted, and Ronde, busted, gave in, handing Tiki the ball.

Tiki wasted no time trying to dribble around Ronde, who was clearly good at defense, even if he did foul frequently. Since there were no free throws in one-on-one, there was no advantage to Tiki drawing further punishment. Instead, he started chucking up shots from all over the court, then trying to outhustle Ronde for any rebounds.

This strategy succeeded in gaining Tiki a 6–3 lead before he hit a dry spell shooting. Ronde doggedly dribbled his way back to 6–5 before their mom forced them to take a dinner break.

They wolfed down their food, washed and dried their dishes, then went straight back out to the driveway to finish their duel.

It was dark out now, and cold, and there were one or two icy patches where yesterday's freezing rain had coated the edge of the driveway. But each of the twins was determined to prove that *he* was the one who deserved the spot on the basketball team.

All of their natural athletic ability was going to waste, now that football season was over, and they both felt the deep need to compete, whatever sport it might be.

It took another fifteen minutes before Tiki finally got his tenth point. Now he had the ball, a 10–7 lead, and a chance to finish Ronde off.

Desperate to put an end to this match before they both froze to death, Tiki put on his best move of the night. Ronde stumbled backward, allowing Tiki a clear path to the basket.

But Tiki had a point to prove. He pulled up and launched a long shot, sinking it off the backboard. Then he turned to Ronde and said, "There. *Now* who says I can't shoot?"

Ronde got up, shook his head, and smiled. "You whupped me, bro. True is true. I guess you *can* shoot some, after all."

"Ha!"

"So . . . I'll take the job at Mr. Landzberg's, and you go on and join the team." Ronde offered his hand, and the twins did their elaborate secret handshake to seal the deal.

"And remember, you promised way back when to help me write that advice column," Tiki reminded him.

Ronde winced, but he knew he was busted. "I *did* say that, didn't I? What was I thinking?"

"I couldn't tell you," Tiki said, grinning. "But a promise is a promise."

"Man, this is not my night," Ronde said with a sigh as they put the ball away and shut the garage door.

"Hey, if it doesn't work out for me, you can take my spot," Tiki offered.

"Don't jinx yourself," said Ronde, clapping him on the back and laughing. "But if you do mess up, you *know* I'll be there, waiting to clean it up for you."

3

THE NEW GUY

"Yoo-hoo! Tiiii-kiii!"

Ronde didn't turn around at first. But when the shrill cooing noise was repeated, more urgently this time, he realized someone had mistaken him for his twin (had to have, because Tiki was at basketball practice).

Ronde sighed wistfully and turned around to correct the mistaken owner of the voice. From down the empty hallway, he saw Laura Sommer leaning out the doorway of the *Hidden Valley Gazette*'s office.

She crooked her finger at him and called, "Have you been avoiding me or something?"

"Me? N-no!" Ronde stammered, walking back down the hall toward her. She remained in the doorway, half in the room and half out, making him cover all the distance.

"Football season's been over for three weeks," Laura said, finally swinging the rest of herself out into the hallway and closing the door behind her. Her voice lowered, so the conversation was just between them. "It's time for you to keep your promise and start writing your fabulous advice column again."

"Listen, I'm—"

"No excuses," Laura said firmly. "I *know* you won't want to break your word . . . and have *everyone* in the whole school *know* it."

"No, you don't understand; I'm not—"

"Are you going to stand there and make excuses, Tiki Barber?"

"I'm RONDE!" he blurted out. "I'm not . . . not Tiki. But I'll *tell* him for you, for sure. No problem."

"Oh, come on, Tiki. Don't pull that stuff with me. As if I didn't know you from your brother."

"Uh . . ."

"I've said what I have to say. I've got a pile of letters for you from last fall. Shall we start with those?"

"I'm *Ronde*. I'm not him. I mean, Tiki. I mean . . ."

"I'll go get them. Stay right where you are—*Tiki*."

Ronde didn't wait for her to come back with the letters. He figured that, since he wasn't Tiki, it wasn't *him* she'd told to stay put—so he was free to go. *Sort* of.

I'd better go warn Tiki, he told himself as he scurried down the stairs, headed for the gym. *And I'm gonna get my hair cut short, too—so people don't get confused between us.*

. . .

"What?!"

Ronde could tell Tiki was annoyed. No, not just annoyed . . . *panicked.*

"I figured she'd come after me in the *spring*, not *now*!" Tiki said, putting both hands on his head. "I've got too much going on right now!"

"So? Just tell her that," said Ronde.

"Oh, right, and have the whole school think I'm welching on a promise. Great. Just great."

"I guess you'll have to tell her the truth and hope she understands."

Ronde knew the minute he said it how ridiculous that sounded. Laura Sommer did not care about Tiki's hoop dreams. The paper was her life, and Tiki had made her a solemn promise.

"I've gotta get to work," Ronde said. "Mr. Landzberg will be waiting for me."

"Okay, thanks," said Tiki. "Wish me luck."

"With Laura?"

"No, man. Here. With the team."

"Sure, but why? What's up?"

"Tell you later. But I'll say one thing, bro—it's not like *our* team."

Ronde thought about Tiki's words as he headed to his first day on the job at Landzberg's Department Store warehouse—which was behind the store itself, on a side street. A bridge connected the two buildings on the fourth floor, so that goods could be brought across, no matter what the weather.

Mr. Landzberg was waiting for him, carrying a clipboard. "Ah, there you are, Ronde. Glad to see you. Nice haircut, by the way."

Ronde ran a hand over his newly shorn head. He'd gotten a buzz cut right after school. Neither Laura Sommer nor anyone else would be mistaking him for Tiki anytime soon.

They shook hands, and Mr. Landzberg put a hand on his shoulder. "I've actually got an errand for you to run, before I even show you around the place."

"Okay," said Ronde, nodding. "What do I do?"

"Run over to this address—it's only a few blocks away—and see what's happened to our other stockboy, Ralph Ramirez. He hasn't shown up for four days in a row, and the home phone's been disconnected." Mr. Landzberg frowned. "I'm a little worried about him. Ralphie's never been irresponsible. I want to know what's going on. So run over there and let me know what's up, okay?"

"Sure thing, Mr. Landzberg," Ronde said, taking the paper with the address and setting off at a run.

"Hey!" Mr. Landzberg called after him, "I didn't mean *run*, run, I meant, just don't go slow. The last thing I need is a stockboy with a twisted ankle."

Ronde grinned, reduced his gait to a trot, and soon found himself at the appointed place. It was an older building, and although there were doorbells in the lobby, the front door wasn't locked. So when there was no answer, Ronde let himself through and walked up the stairs to apartment 2B, where he knocked on the door.

At first, no one answered. "Hello?" Ronde called out loudly. "I'm here from Mr. Landzberg!"

Suddenly, the door swung open, and a tall, skinny kid of about sixteen stared back at him. "Sorry," he said. "I thought it might be the landlord."

"Huh?"

"We haven't paid the rent, and we're afraid if we answer the door, it will be trouble."

"Oh. So, you're . . ." He checked the paper Mr. Landzberg had given him. "Ralph?"

"That's me," the kid said without smiling.

"Ronde. Ronde Barber," he said, offering his hand. Ralph just stared at it.

"Um, do you mind if I ask you a question?" Ronde wondered.

Ralph blinked, then shook his head. "What?"

"If you need rent, how come you aren't coming to work?"

The boy sighed, and gestured over his shoulder. "My

ma is sick in bed," he said sadly. "I've gotta take care of her. We've got nobody else . . . except my aunt, and she can come only once a week."

"Is your mom . . . is she gonna be all right?" Ronde asked in a near whisper.

The boy swallowed hard. "She says so . . . but I don't know. She doesn't tell me everything."

"I'm . . . I'm sorry," Ronde said. "I . . . I hope she feels better. I'll tell Mr. Landzberg what you said."

"Thanks," said Ralph, and closed the door.

As he walked, not ran, back to the store, Ronde thought how lucky he and Tiki were. Sure, their mom had to work long hours—but at least she was *healthy*. Whatever problems he and Tiki had, other people had harder things to deal with, by far.

An hour ago, Ronde had been in agony over losing his one-on-one battle with Tiki and having to go to work, while Tiki got to be on the b-ball team. Now, Ronde was thrilled to be able to work and help his family. It was the least he could do to show his gratitude for all the blessings life had given him.

4

GAME ON!

At that same moment, Tiki was busy at practice, where things were not going so well. Even before Ronde had come to the gym to warn him that Laura Sommer was after him to honor his commitment, Tiki had been having a hard time.

While everything here was new to him, it was already midseason for the rest of the team. And Coach Jackson was nothing like Sam Wheeler, who ran the football team as if he were the general of an elite strike force.

Jackson was much more laid-back. He let the players go through their paces with just a hint of direction here and there. That left practice in the hands of Sugar Morton, the team's shooting guard, and therefore, its on-court general.

Sugar was not laid-back in the least. His personality was dominating, and his huge natural talent for the game helped give him even more authority over his teammates.

Today, that authority was being put to use mostly to help Rory Mathis, the substitute shooting guard who was now going to be starting, go through the team's set plays with the rest of the starting five.

Tiki knew this drill. It was hard for a kid who was used to subbing to suddenly have all the focus put on him, and Rory was no exception. He knew, as they all did, that Brian Reynolds, who had been shipped off to military school, was a better shooter. That was why, until now, Rory had sat on the bench most of the time.

Tiki, the new sub, was not the priority at the moment. He was left pretty much on his own, to watch, and learn the plays.

Coach Wheeler would have given him a book full of diagrams to study, but Coach Jackson was not like that. It had never occurred to him that once he'd taught the team the plays, he might need to show them to new players in the middle of the season.

Tiki figured out the five-man weave pretty quickly, and managed to draw a few appreciative comments when he got his turn to be a part of it.

The other plays were much harder, though. One, called Brooklyn, was designed to clear out the right side of the frontcourt so Sugar could go one-on-one with his defender. Tiki caught on to that one pretty fast too.

As for the rest, he soon found his head buzzing. He wished he'd brought a pad and paper with him to diagram the plays for himself, but he'd never thought the coach wouldn't have handouts to give him!

Afterward, in the locker room, when Coach Jackson clapped him on the shoulder and thanked him for joining the team, Tiki didn't mention his confusion. He was embarrassed to admit that he hadn't really caught on to most of it.

Besides, from what he and Ronde had witnessed the other day at the game, the team didn't use most of those plays much anyway. More often than not, it was just Sugar Morton playing his brand of amazing street b-ball, against whoever and whatever the other team threw at him. So Tiki figured it wouldn't really matter much if he didn't know the plays when game time rolled around.

As it happened, his first game was the very next day. He'd had no time to think about what to tell Laura Sommer, but he figured he could avoid her until he'd at least had some game action under his belt. Twice that day, he'd had to duck into stairwells to keep her from spotting him in the halls. As soon as the final bell rang, Tiki raced down the stairs to the locker room, his book bag tucked under his arm like a football.

This was a familiar drill to him. This felt right. This

was the feeling he'd missed all these weeks since the football season had ended—the feeling of his blood coursing through him, his heart pumping, his breathing deep and fast.

He burst into the locker room, where he expected to find the rest of the team as excited as he was. Instead, he saw a group of boys sitting casually on benches, or combing their hair in the mirror, or slowly getting into uniform, expressionless.

"Wuzzup!" he greeted them, but the most he got in reply were a few "hey"s. Everyone seemed to be feeling down, and it took Tiki only a moment to realize why.

Brian Reynolds, their normal starting shooting guard, was gone for the season. Their record was a game under .500. And their coach wasn't even there!

"Mr. Jackson's got a teachers' meeting," explained Bobby Dominic, the team's starting center. Bobby was about six feet tall, maybe even taller. He was skinny as a stick, and his arms looked like branches waving in the breeze.

Not much muscle on him, Tiki couldn't help noticing. In spite of his height, Bobby had gotten pushed around by the other team's center and forwards during the game he and Ronde had watched.

Would today be any different?

"Time to get out there," Sugar said, and they all rose as one. It was, Tiki observed, as if the coach himself had spoken. They filed into the gym, slowly, like prisoners going to the gallows.

Tiki had to shake his head. He couldn't wait to get into his first game on the basketball team! It was hard for him to believe that he was the only one who cared that much.

Coach Jackson arrived on the scene right before tip-off. "Okay," he told the players as they gathered around him. "Pulaski's a tough team, and we're in transition. But let's at least try to put up a good fight. You never know what might happen. Give it your best, guys!"

Tiki couldn't believe it! Coach Wheeler would have exploded in rage. How could the coach not even *try* to inspire his team? Did he think they'd already lost, or what?

Tiki started the game on the bench, but right from the opening tip-off, he was itching to get out there and be a part of the action.

At first, things went well. Sugar hit a couple of easy shots, and Bobby blocked a shot by the Wildcats' power forward.

But then, things started to turn sour. Rory Mathis missed his first two jumpers, and committed a couple of quick fouls. Only four minutes in, and Tiki found himself coming into the game!

He looked over to the stands, trying to spot Ronde. There was his twin, jumping up and down and screaming something encouraging. Tiki smiled and waved.

"Okay, Mr. Football, let's see what you've got," Sugar said, slapping him on the back.

Mr. Football? Tiki thought it was a strange thing to call him—and he wasn't very happy about it, either. He was trying to think of himself as a basketball player right now, not a football star.

Tiki inbounded the ball to Sugar, who dribbled downcourt. By now, the Wildcat defenders had figured out that they needed to double-team the Eagles' star. Cornered, Sugar dished off to Tiki at the head of the foul circle.

Tiki felt overcome with excitement—he was free, and had the ball! Squaring himself to the basket, he launched a long shot. *SWISH!!* A three-pointer!

"Yeah!" yelled Bobby Dominic, high-fiving Tiki on their way back upcourt. Sugar was clapping his hands too. Tiki gave them a little wave and a nod. He felt fantastic.

Now the Wildcats came slowly upcourt, launching a set play. Tiki's man was shorter than he was, but he had a quick set of moves, and an even quicker shot. Before he could stop the kid, he dribbled around Tiki and put up an easy ten-footer for two points.

"Man!" Tiki said, shaking his head. He knew he had to do better on defense against such a quick opponent.

Again, Sugar Morton found himself surrounded by

Pulaski defenders. Again, he found Tiki at the point. Again, Tiki launched a long bomb, and again—*SWISH!*

"Wow!" Tiki heard Coach Jackson yelling. "We've got us a player! Yeah, baby!"

Tiki felt great—until his man faked him out, pulled back, and nailed a three-pointer of his own.

Well, so far, we're even, just about, thought Tiki. But he knew in his heart that his first two shots had been lucky. Ronde hadn't been that far wrong when he'd said they weren't great shooters.

This time down the court, Sugar tried forcing his way through the defense, and was stripped of the ball. The fast break happened so quickly that Tiki was caught off guard. His man put in an easy layup, and Pulaski took the lead for the first time in the game.

"*Defense,* yo!" Sugar yelled at Tiki as they headed back downcourt. "You've gotta play both ends of the court!"

Tiki nodded, showing he understood. But he could feel the blood rush to his face. He wanted to answer Sugar back. In fact, he would have liked to answer with his fists. But he knew he couldn't. Fists never solved anything, and this was not the time to get into a war of words with the leader of the team.

And there was no doubt Sugar was their leader. The other kids looked to *him,* not their coach, for direction. The problem was, as Tiki well knew, it's impossible to play and coach at the same time.

Sugar was being swarmed by the Wildcats now. They could see how determined he was to dominate the game, and they were just as determined to shut him down, and make the rest of the Eagles do the scoring.

Sugar dished off to Tiki, who turned and launched another shot—but this time, his defender was ready. For a short kid, he sure could jump, thought Tiki after seeing his shot batted away.

"Don't shoot if you're not free!" Sugar yelled at him as they retreated back upcourt. "Who do you think you are, Michael Jordan?"

Tiki had to bite down hard on his lip to keep from saying something he knew he'd regret. But he was determined to show Sugar that he was a good player who deserved respect.

The next two times he touched the ball, Tiki put up shots he probably shouldn't have. He wasn't open either time, and he missed the basket by a lot. Tiki gritted his teeth to keep from hearing whatever Sugar was shouting at him.

For their part, Pulaski kept running their set plays—playing pick-and-roll and finding open shots nearly every time down the court. Soon, they had built up a double-digit lead. Coach Jackson had to call time-out to stop the bleeding.

In the huddle, though, it was Sugar who did most of the talking. "That's it!" he said hotly. "You guys are just standing around out there. Barber's the only one who's getting open—and all he wants to do is shoot!"

Again, Tiki had to stop himself from an ill-timed outburst. But he promised himself that he would talk to Sugar, man to man, face to face, at the first opportune moment.

"From now on," Sugar told Tiki as they headed back onto the floor, "just quit shooting and pass it back to me."

"But—" This time, Tiki couldn't help himself from responding. But it was too late. Sugar was already running out onto the court, and couldn't hear him over the roar of the crowd in the bleachers.

Looking behind him, Tiki saw Coach Jackson looking at him. Had he heard what Sugar had said? If so, he gave no sign of it. Even if he had, he'd chosen not to say anything.

Tiki couldn't believe how different Coach Jackson was from Coach Wheeler. He remembered how Wheeler had dealt with Cody Hansen when the quarterback had gotten out of hand. He'd reamed him out—in private, to be sure—but Cody had changed his ways from that point on. And the team had responded with a winning streak.

Tiki wondered if the same thing could ever happen here. Sugar Morton was as talented as any athlete at Hidden Valley, Tiki and Ronde included. But he had an attitude you could cut with a knife, and it was killing his team's spirit.

"Just pass the ball back to Sugar," Tiki heard some-one mutter in his ear. Turning, he saw it was Bobby Dominic. "I know it bites," Bobby said, "but you're bet-ter off keeping it inside. You don't know what he's like when he's angry."

Tiki was about to say something in reply, but the whistle blew and Bobby had to get back out onto the court.

Tiki began the second half where he'd begun the first—on the bench. He watched as Sugar put on a one-man show, same as he'd done the previous game. When the Wildcats double-teamed and triple-teamed him, he drew a foul and sank the free throws. He did everything to keep his team in the game—except share the ball.

As for Rory, he managed to stay out of foul trouble during the second half, so Tiki only got into the game for a few minutes. During his time on the court, he was afraid to shoot, lest he miss again and get yelled at by Sugar in front of everyone.

As in the previous game, this one ended with the Eagles on the losing end—54–48. Sugar Morton had racked up thirty-one points, but it wasn't nearly enough.

Maybe if he hadn't fouled out, called for charging with two minutes left to play, he might have managed to somehow put them over the top. Instead, Sugar raged from the bench at the referee, who rang him up for a technical foul on top of it.

"Same old story," Tiki heard Bobby mutter as the team shuffled out of the gym, heads hanging.

In the locker room, things were tense. Larry Budnick, the starting small forward, started grumbling about how few touches he'd had during the game. "I might have taken two whole shots the entire game," summed up what he had to say.

"Took two shots, hit how many, Budnick?" Sugar shot back, not even bothering to look at Larry. "Maybe if you were a better shooter, I'd get you more touches."

"Maybe if I got to take enough shots to get into a rhythm . . ." Larry countered.

"You need rhythm, go take some dancing lessons," Sugar barked, in a tone that said, *This conversation is over*.

Tiki stayed out of it, though he would have liked to offer Larry some support. But he knew there was no point in arguing with people like Sugar. Once they were already emotional, they never changed their minds or listened to reason.

Hmmm . . . , he said to himself. *Might make a good advice column. . . .*

He filed the thought away and waited for the locker room to empty out.

"So long, Barber," said Sugar, giving him a little punch in the arm. "Not bad for your first game. Keep working it."

After all the other players had gone, Coach Jackson gave Tiki a long look. *"What?"* he finally asked. "What's on your mind, Tiki? Got something to ask me?"

"Kind of," Tiki said sheepishly. "I mean, you're the coach, and I'm just new here, but . . ."

"Yes?" Jackson prompted. "I'm the coach . . . and . . . ?"

"Well, that's kind of the *point*, sort of," Tiki went on, meeting Jackson's gaze. *"You're* the one in charge."

"It's not easy," Jackson said slowly, sighed, and sat down on the bench next to Tiki. "Thing is, kid, you don't know Sugar. He's really, REALLY difficult to deal with."

"But it's killing the team's spirit!" Tiki blurted out. *There, he'd said it.* "They don't even act like teammates!"

Coach Jackson shrugged, shaking his head. "I know. I can see that. I'm not blind, in spite of what you might think. And it's not like I haven't *tried* talking to him. I'm just not getting through."

Tiki wanted to say, *You* couldn't *have talked to him—not the right way, anyway! Coach Wheeler would know how to get through to a kid like Sugar.*

But he didn't say that. There would have been no point. What could Jackson do about the fact that he wasn't Coach Wheeler?

Nothing, that's what.

"Frankly, I can't control him," the coach confessed. "And to be completely honest with you, I am under pressure."

"From where?" Tiki wasn't sure what Coach Jackson meant.

"The principal, the parents, the kids—everyone!" Jackson shook his head. "You know, last season he was a different animal. That's because we had Eli Raines."

Tiki remembered Raines, star of last year's basketball team. He'd been a six-foot-two center who was built like a fortress—as unlike Bobby Dominic as two centers could be. He'd also had a terrific short jumper and a decent three-point shot.

"As long as Raines was around, Sugar was always in check. Seems like he didn't learn anything about leadership from Eli. The minute it was his turn, Sugar turned into a 'star.' Now, suddenly, it's all about him instead of the team! And what am I supposed to do, bench him? He's more than half our scoring, for goodness' sake! Dr. Anand would have my head, and so would the whole student body!"

Dr. Anand was the school's principal. Tiki knew how much pride she took in everything good about the school. Every time one of her students excelled, she made sure it was celebrated and talked about, even in the *Roanoke Reporter*.

Tiki could see what kind of a pickle Coach Jackson was in, all right. No matter what he did, someone was going to be mad at him. And some people just can't take people being mad at them.

"Tiki, to be honest, that's why *you're* here."

That got Tiki's attention. "Huh?"

"I didn't just bring you onto the squad for your basketball skills—although I thought you played very well today, considering it was your first game."

"Thanks."

"But I really brought you here for two other reasons. One, as I told Ronde, was the inspiration factor. You guys know how to win, and you're proven leaders. But the other reason is that I thought . . . well . . . maybe you'd serve as an example to Sugar. After all, you and Ronde are even more popular around the school than he is. I figured maybe he'd listen to one of you."

"What can I do?" Tiki said, aghast.

"Maybe talk to him. Player to player. Well, not yet," Jackson said. "Not until you've got your game going on. He's not going to listen to anyone who's not playing all that well."

"Huh? I thought you said I *did* play well!"

"For your first game, yes. But you took a few shots you shouldn't have, and you've got to be quicker on defense. Shape up your game for next time, and then maybe Sugar will listen to you."

He clapped Tiki on the knee. "So between now and next game, let's you and me work on your defense, huh?"

5

THE OTHER BROTHER

Ronde was pushing as hard as he could, and still, the hand truck with boxes piled on it barely moved. Ronde tried again. This time it got going, slowly at first, then more easily as he pushed and guided it down the aisle of the warehouse.

Work was *hard*! He hadn't fully realized it until now.

Tiki still couldn't understand, because he'd never had to work at a job like this. Writing an advice column for the school paper might qualify as work, but that was only your *brain* working. This was your *body and brain together*—your body to lift the boxes and push the hand truck or dolly, and the brains to figure out from the order list which boxes to take off the shelves, and where to bring them.

It was a relief for Ronde whenever Mr. Landzberg

called him aside and gave him an envelope or package to take over to Ralphie's house. Ronde never opened them to see what they contained, but he was pretty sure the envelopes held cash for the Ramirez family, who were going through such hard times.

Mr. Landzberg is a really nice guy, thought Ronde. He knew that not all bosses were nice, because some of his mom's bosses had been, as she'd put it, "a real pain."

Whenever he got one of these errands to do, Ronde felt free and happy. Sure, he was working, but this was fun, too—running down the street, dodging imaginary obstacles, holding the imaginary "football." During their time on the Eagles, it was always Tiki who'd gotten to run with the ball. So it was fun to pretend, and try out his best moves on pedestrians, pets, and lampposts alike.

"Thanks, Ronde," Ralphie would say as he took the envelope.

"How's your mom?" Ronde would always ask.

"About the same" or "not too great today" or occasionally, "pretty good" would come the reply. And Ronde always felt good to be bringing some cheer to that home.

So far, he'd been at his job almost two weeks. And all that time, Tiki had been practicing and playing with the team. But today's contest against the East

Side Mountaineers was the first time since Tiki's first game that Ronde was going to be able to attend. Thursday was Ralphie's day to work, because on Thursdays, his aunt was able to come over and watch his mom for a while.

Ronde got to the gym early and found a seat just behind the home team's bench. He was right there to high-five the players as they came in from the locker room. "Play proud, bro," he told Tiki, using their mom's favorite saying.

Tiki nodded back superconfidently—as if he could fool his own identical twin. Ronde knew very well how nervous Tiki had become about his role on the team. Like many identical twins, he could almost feel his twin's feelings as if they were his own.

Ronde expected there to be a coach's pep talk, complete with team cheer. But aside from a half-baked huddle, and Coach Jackson saying "Let's go get 'em," there was nothing. No hands over hands, no "YEAH!!" no excitement at all.

Only Sugar seemed revved up to go, clapping his hands vigorously and staring intently at his teammates. Tiki was silent, frowning, alone with his own thoughts, except that Ronde could read them like a book.

From the opening tip-off, the Eagles found themselves outplayed. The East Side Mountaineers were smaller, but they were also faster, and they clearly wanted this game more than the home team.

At least that was how it looked to Ronde, who had a bird's eye view of the game from his second-row seat. "Let's go!" he called out through cupped hands. "Let's get it going, now!"

It was the same kind of game he'd seen the last time. Tiki had been with the team for two weeks, and they looked as scrappy as ever.

Not that Sugar wasn't turning in his usual stellar performance. He sank four jumpers in a row to tie the score at 22. But nobody else got to be a part of the offense, and when he sat down for a breather late in the first half, the team hit a wall. For the rest of the half, all they scored was two points on a couple of free throws.

Tiki hadn't played much—maybe two or three minutes in total. But during that whole stint, Sugar had passed him the ball only once. And Tiki was supposed to be the team's shooting guard!

What good is a shooting guard if you don't get him the ball to shoot? Ronde asked himself. But he had no good answer.

Sure, Morton's total of eighteen points looked good for one half. Ronde could understand why Sugar thought that, where Eagle scoring was concerned, it was him or nothing.

At the start of the second half, though, Sugar was ice-cold, his shots rimming out, or missing entirely.

After four or five bricks, the home crowd started growing restless.

Ronde could tell that Tiki was getting frustrated too. The coach had put him in for the start of the half— an upgrade, for sure, Ronde noted with pride in his brother.

But as he also knew from their time on the football team, Tiki was used to *holding the ball*. It couldn't have been easy for him to keep silent about Sugar's ball-hogging, the way Bobby Dominic did.

After one play where Tiki had been free and yelling for the ball, waving his hands only to have Sugar ignore him and put up another brick, Tiki groaned out loud and grabbed his head with both hands. While he was distracted, his man blew by him on his way downcourt to catch a long lob pass and lay it in!

"Wake up, Barber!" Morton barked at him.

Ronde saw that Tiki was about to explode. Luckily, at just that moment, the whistle blew across court, where the center, Bobby Dominic, had fouled one of the Mountaineers.

Coach Jackson called Tiki over to the bench, sending Rory Mathis out to replace him.

"You've got to control yourself better than that," Ronde heard Coach Jackson tell his twin.

"But—"

"I know," Jackson stopped him. "But during the

game is not the time to take it up with him."

Ronde leaned forward, hearing all this. After Coach Jackson had turned his back, he put a hand on Tiki's shoulder and whispered in his ear, "Hang in there, bro."

Tiki snorted angrily. "Yeah, right," he muttered. "Thanks, though. Appreciate the support."

"No problem. I've got your back."

Ronde went back to watching the game, but it was more of the same. Finally, with less than five minutes left and the Eagles down by almost twenty points, the coach sent Tiki back in there.

Ronde could tell that his brother was steaming mad. He wondered how Tiki would handle all that anger on the court. Would he be able to use it—or would his anger handle *him*?

Soon, Ronde had his answer. Off a rebound, Tiki got open, and Bobby Dominic got him the ball. He tossed up a three-pointer, and *SWISH*!

Ronde and the rest of the crowd whooped it up— especially when, seconds later, Tiki recovered a loose ball and found Sugar open for another three!

The rest of the Eagles seemed suddenly inspired. Bobby blocked a shot, and it came right to Tiki, who dribbled upcourt, and found Sugar open again. He buried the shot, and suddenly, they were only eleven points down, with four minutes still to play.

The Mountaineers called time, and the Eagles

huddled up. Ronde leaned forward to listen in. "Sugar," Coach J said. "You okay?"

Sugar was breathing hard, his hands on his hips. He nodded, but said nothing. Ronde wondered if Sugar had enough wind to say a word. He looked totally gassed, and why wouldn't he be? Coach Jackson hadn't sat him down once the whole game!

Had Jackson noticed how exhausted Sugar was? If he had, he gave no sign, just clapping his hands and saying, "Okay, we've got 'em right where we want 'em! Let's go get 'em!"

Oh, well, thought Ronde. At least the coach sounded excited—and why shouldn't he be? His team was back in the game, if only just. And he had himself a real star player, who lit up the scoreboard every single game. Sugar Morton was practically a living highlight reel!

The game resumed, and the Eagles kept storming back. With just under a minute left in, they regained possession of the ball in their own end. Sugar dribbled upcourt, his eyes scanning the defense. Tiki ran alongside him on the far side of the court, open for a pass in case the Mountaineers double-teamed Sugar.

They did, soon enough, but instead of passing the ball to Tiki, Sugar tried to bull his way through them. He drew a foul, and sank both free throws. Only one point now separated the teams as the Mountaineers came back upcourt with the ball.

Tiki guarded his man tightly, not letting him get close to the basket when he had possession.

Then, with twenty seconds left, Ronde saw that Tiki could steal the ball if he left his man and got into the passing lane. He wished he could yell to Tiki to get there . . . !

No need. Identical twins think alike. Just as if Ronde had willed it, or sent Tiki a message by mental telepathy, Tiki dropped off his man and dove for the pass—

Except the pass never came. The point guard for the Mountaineers must have seen Tiki's eyes, and known he was coming. He held on to the ball instead of passing it. Tiki's man was now free at the basket. An easy lob resulted in a crushing layup—all because Tiki had blown his coverage!

Ronde saw Sugar yell something at Tiki, but he couldn't make out the words over the groan of the home crowd. Now the Eagles were down by three again, with only fourteen seconds left, and no time-outs.

Tiki loped upcourt, shaking his head and looking at the ground. Sugar dribbled to half-court, then tried to slice through the defense to get at the basket.

There was no thought of dishing out to the free man at the point or in the corners. Sugar was going to take it to the hoop himself, and everybody knew it—including the defenders. The shot was swatted away like a lazy fly—and the ball landed in *Tiki's hands*!

There he was, with an open shot! The crowd was screaming now, and Ronde saw Sugar calling for the ball. The clock ticked down to two seconds . . . one second . . .

Tiki launched the ball just as the defender got his hand up. It sailed, arcing high, and hit the far rim before bouncing straight up in the air. It came down again, hitting the rim a second time before dropping to the ground as the buzzer sounded, breaking the hearts of the Eagles and their fans.

The crowd fell eerily silent. And in the silence, Ronde, and everyone else, heard Sugar Morton's voice ring out: *"Barber! What were you thinking?"*

Ronde knew exactly what Tiki had been thinking. There had been no time to pass the ball—only time to throw up one last, desperate prayer. And that was exactly what Tiki had done!

But Tiki said nothing. He strode silently toward the locker room. Ronde could almost see the steam shooting out of his brother's ears.

6

SOME SAGE ADVICE

"You mean to say you never said anything? NOTHING??"

Tiki frowned. "Don't stare at me like that, Ronde. You wouldn't have either."

"As if! I would totally have said something! I'd have knocked his block off!"

Tiki sniggered. "Yeah, right, Ronde. When's the last time you ever even shoved anybody—except me, that is?"

Ronde furrowed his brows in thought, but he needn't have bothered.

"Never, that's when," Tiki said triumphantly. "So don't go saying things about what I should have or could have done in that locker room."

Ronde sighed. "I guess you're right. But how could you not have at least said something to him?"

"*Think,* dude," Tiki said. He'd been pacing the room,

but now sat down next to Ronde on the edge of the couch. "What would have happened if I'd done that?"

Ronde grinned. "A fight?"

"Yeah, you'd *better* smile when you say that," Tiki said, grinning himself. "You know it would have been a bad scene. The team would have fallen apart right then and there."

"It's not much of a team as it is," Ronde pointed out.

"True. *Somebody* should sure say *something* to Sugar."

"Coach Jackson said that's why you're on the team, right?"

"Well, he's got the wrong guy," Tiki said, shaking his head. "I'm not the type to go head-to-head and have it out with somebody. I didn't even do that with Cody, and that was the *football* team!"

He got up and started pacing again. "This just isn't working out," he said. "I thought being on the b-ball team would be fun, you know?"

"Well, maybe you've got to give it more time," Ronde suggested. "It's only been two weeks."

"Yeah, but I can see already where the rest of the season is headed," Tiki replied. "I just don't know, Ronde." He fell silent for a moment. "Maybe . . ." he began, then fell silent again.

"Maybe *what*?"

"You know, I took the spot on the team because I'm a better shooter than you. . . ."

"Hey!"

"Don't argue. I won that game of one-on-one, so the issue is decided. But the point is, I'm not getting the chance to shoot very much. So what good am I doing there? Like I said, I'm not going to be able to put Sugar in his place."

"Are you saying . . . ?"

"How about switching with me? I mean, you're better than me at defense, at least. And if we're not going to be shooting . . ."

"I get your point," Ronde said. "But I don't know . . . I'm not exactly the type to go head-to-head with that kid either."

"Hey, you can't do any less good than I'm doing— which is *none*."

"You know what, though?" Ronde said. "It might be good for you to take on the job at Landzberg's. I mean, then you could tell Laura you haven't got time to write the advice column."

"That's true!" Tiki said, suddenly brightening. "So, is it a deal?"

"You bet!" Ronde said, and they exchanged their secret handshake to seal the deal. "So, who's gonna break the news to Coach Jackson?"

. . .

The coach was happy enough to make the switch. "As far as I'm concerned, either one of you guys is a better bet than anybody else at the school," he said. "You're both terrific athletes, and the more you play basketball, the more comfortable you'll be on the court. I'm only sorry I couldn't play you as my starter, Tiki."

"Oh, no, I understand," said Tiki sincerely. "I'm just the new guy. Rory's been on the team all season."

"And the season before that," Coach added. "And that whole time, he's come off the bench. So this is his chance, and I can't take that away from him."

"Totally," said Ronde.

"Of course," Tiki agreed. They'd both ridden the bench during their first season on the football team, and they understood what it was like—how much you yearned to get out there and show everyone what you were capable of.

"Besides," Coach Jackson said, leaning back in his chair as he sat across the desk from them, "it's not like anybody gets to take a lot of shots, other than Sugar."

"Ever think of making him the shooting guard?" Ronde wondered. "I mean, shooting is what he does, and he's really good at it too."

"But he's also my best ball-handler, by far," Jackson said. "Rory Nelson is my sub at point guard. He's a seventh grader, and he is still working on having a feel for the position, it seems."

Tiki realized suddenly what should have been obvious to him all along. Not all coaches had a team full of talented players, the way Coach Wheeler did. They'd been lucky in that way. Even the seventh-graders had talent on those Eagles. This basketball team had a lot of talent, but most of it was Sugar's.

"So look, Ronde, I'll need you at practice tomorrow, to break you in and show you the set plays and defenses," said Jackson. "Tiki . . . thanks for everything. And anytime you want to switch back, that's okay too. You did a fine job. . . ."

. . . *for a guy who's never been on a basketball team before, except for pickup games at the playground,* thought Tiki as he shook the coach's hand. "Thanks, Coach. I enjoyed it . . . *most* of it."

From that moment on, Tiki was a working man, and Ronde was a ballplayer. You would have thought Ronde would be the happy one, but looking over at him, Tiki saw that he was deep in thought. Ronde seemed worried, and he could imagine why.

Curiously, Tiki was the one who felt much better as they walked away from the coach's office. It was like a weight had been removed from his shoulders. He wondered how Ronde would bear that burden, now that it was his.

. . .

"There's this kid at work—Ralphie?" Ronde said as they lay in their beds in the darkened bedroom that night. "His mom's really sick, and has been for a long time. He can't come in to work except for one day a week, but Mr. L. sends the family money and stuff."

"So? Why're you telling me?"

"Mr. L. will want you to deliver the stuff to the kid's house."

"Oh." Tiki stared up at the ceiling and the dozens of stick-on, glow-in-the-dark stars he and Ronde had put up there. They glowed down on the boys now, like constellations in the night sky.

"I just thought you should know."

"Why?"

"Well, it's just . . . every time I go over there, I get all sad and stuff. Some people are really struggling with a lot of hard things. . . . And we're real lucky, you know?"

"Uh-huh." Tiki wondered what he was getting at.

"I was just thinking," Ronde said. "You know Sugar?"

"Of course I know him, duh. What's he got to do with it?"

"I don't know . . . but like, when Ralphie's mom first got sick—before he started not being able to work—he told me he used to get angry all the time. Sometimes he'd go nuts for a minute, and do something crazy like break a dish or yell at his dog. You know?"

"Whoa," said Tiki softly. "That's some bad stuff, all right. So you're saying . . . ?"

"Well, what if *that's* what's going on with *Sugar*? I mean, Coach said that last year he was a team player, and how he never thought Sean would turn into a star-type."

"That's true—Coach said he couldn't talk to him anymore; that he wouldn't listen."

Tiki was deep in thought now. Maybe Ronde was on to something. If something was going on with Sean Morton that he couldn't talk to anybody about, that might explain his hostile behavior.

"Maybe you should try to find out what's really up with him," Tiki suggested. "I mean, now that you're on the team and all. He doesn't hate you yet, the way he does me. . . ."

"Come on, he does not hate you!"

"Well, he acts like he hates the whole rest of the team. You'd think we were letting him down or something, but it's not like we're not trying. . . ." Tiki thought about that for a moment. "And even if some of the guys *aren't* trying hard all the time, who could blame them? The way Sugar hogs the ball, they might as well be doing something else, 'cause they're not in the game, really. At least not on offense."

He looked over at Ronde, both of them lying under the same glowing stars. "Maybe you're right," he said.

"Maybe there's something we don't know about Sugar that's making him act like such a brat. And maybe you can find out—if you can keep him from hating you, too."

"I'm gonna try to stay on his good side," Ronde said. "At least for starters."

They lay there for another quiet moment. Then Ronde said, "You know, it's too bad you're not gonna do the column. You could have given Sugar some really good advice."

"Ha! As if he'd ever ask for my advice!"

That was the end of their conversation that night. But long after he'd heard Ronde's soft snoring, Tiki lay awake, thinking.

It's true, he thought. Sugar Morton would never write a letter asking for Tiki's response. But maybe, just maybe, there was another way. . . .

Dear Tiki:

I don't know what to do, but I thought maybe you could help me with my problem. There is this kid, who's in this kind of group with me, and instead of being part of the group, he's always going off and doing stuff on his own, and leaving us out. It's depressing, and it's like he thinks we can't do anything right. Me and my friends are all depressed and angry, but we can't say anything to him, because he shouts us down, and he's like the boss of the group, so there's no use arguing with him. Even the teacher who's our advisor lets him get away with everything because he likes the work this kid does. But the rest of us feel like quitting the group. What should we do?

Signed,

Tiki thought for a moment, then signed the letter *"Perplexed."* He took it with him to school that day.

Laura Sommer saw him in the hall between third and fourth period and yelled, "Don't try slipping away again, Tiki! I know what game you're playing!"

Tiki did not try to run away this time. He let her catch him, saying, "Oh, hi, Laura—I've been meaning to talk to you."

"Sure you have," she said, frowning. "Like I don't know what you've been up to. But that's okay, I've got you now. And there are sixteen letters in my desk for you, all asking for your advice. How soon can you get on it?"

"Uh, sorry, but I've already got my first letter to answer," Tiki said, taking out of his pocket the note signed *"Perplexed."* "This one," he said, "is kind of urgent. I'll have the response for you by Monday."

"Oh!" she said, taking the envelope he'd handed her. "Great! Can't wait! Bye!"

Now all he had to do was figure out what he was going to write. All he knew was, whatever he wound up saying, it had better speak right to Sugar Morton.

7

SUGAR'S DARK SECRET

Ronde was sweating bullets. He tried to shake the stinging droplets out of his eyes without using his hands, which were busy guarding Sugar.

It was exhausting trying to stay with him—all season long, players from other teams had struggled to do it, even in a double-team—but so far, Ronde was hanging in there. He hadn't allowed Sugar a decent shot the whole scrimmage.

"Back off, Barber!" Sugar said, the tendons in his neck stretched tight with tension. "Or you're gonna get knocked over."

"I can take it, if you can dish it out," Ronde shot back.

He instantly regretted his words. If he wanted to make friends with Sugar, to get under his defensive armor, this was no way to get acquainted.

"Whatever. Your funeral," Sugar said, then dashed to his left, so fast that most defenders would have been left standing there.

But not Ronde. His coverage instincts had been honed over three years on the football team as its star cornerback. Sugar was good—as good as anybody Ronde had faced in his years on the Eagles. But he wasn't going to get around Ronde that easily.

"Foul!" Sugar yelled when Ronde blocked his desperate shot.

"I never touched you, man," Ronde said. "But hey, whatever."

"Don't 'whatever' me, Barber," Morton said, turning more serious. The game went on around them until Coach Jackson blew the whistle, clapping his hands for the others to stop.

"Hey, you two!" he called out. "Get your heads back in the game!"

"Sorry, man," Ronde said, offering Sugar his hand to shake. "My bad."

Sugar cocked his head to one side and squinted at Ronde. *He knows I didn't foul him,* Ronde thought. *He's wondering why I'm letting him get away with it. . . .*

They both took off down the court, back into the scrimmage. Ronde didn't show his satisfaction, but he was smiling on the inside. He'd thrown Sugar off-balance. The kid didn't know what to make of him, and that was a good thing. Next step was to get to know Sugar *off the court.*

Ronde was just hoisting his backpack, having showered and changed after practice, when Sugar approached him. "Hey, you've got some game, you know it? You're a lot better player than your brother."

Ronde's first reaction was automatic—to defend Tiki. But he stopped himself. If he wanted this kid to open up to him, he couldn't be constantly arguing with him. "I'm a defensive specialist, I guess you could say," he replied.

Sugar smiled. "Tiki can't play defense worth a dime. Plus he's streaky on offense."

Ronde shook his head and laughed that comment off. "I've seen him go on some pretty good streaks when he gets going." Left unsaid was the obvious—that Tiki would never get any kind of streak going on a team where he had to wait for Sugar to give him the ball.

"He's not a team player," Sugar went on. "But I can see how you're gonna fit right in around here."

Not a team player???

Several images rushed at Ronde all at once—times when Tiki's unselfishness as a player had saved the Eagles from disaster. If anyone wasn't a team player, it was Sugar! Talk about the pot calling the kettle black!

"Hey, you taking the late bus home?"

"Yeah, why?"

"Come on, I'll sit with you."

They walked out to the car park together and got on the bus. "I live over by Exeter Street," Sugar said.

"Yeah? That's only five blocks from us!" Ronde said, surprised. "How did I not know that?"

"Well, I . . ."

"I mean, I *never* see you on the bus. I know I'm absentminded sometimes, but I don't think I could have missed you three years in a row!"

"I, uh . . ." Sugar suddenly fell silent. Then, just as quickly, he changed the subject. "You know what's wrong with this team?"

"Me? No! I mean, how would I know? I just got here!"

If Ronde protested a bit too much, it was because he knew *exactly* what was wrong with the basketball Eagles. He was looking at him right now!

"Well, let me save you the time and effort," said Sugar as they started up the staircase that led from field level, where the gym and locker rooms were, to the main floor, and the doors that led to the parking lot. "I'll tell you what the problem is—it's that everybody's just standing around, waiting for me to make a play."

Finally, Ronde could agree with something Sugar said, and wholeheartedly. "You may be right about that. I did see Bobby and Rory kind of dogging it today. But why do you think they do that?" he asked, trying to draw Sugar out.

"They're just wimps, that's all!" Sugar ranted.

Ronde could feel his anger. Sugar was almost shaking with rage at the thought of it. "I get double-teamed every time, and nobody's willing to put a body on anyone! They could slam me to the ground, and none of those chickens would stick up for me."

That's because they've had it with you, dude, thought Ronde. *Maybe you should be nicer to them; even get them the ball once in a while.*

Of course, he didn't say any of that—that would have been the end of the conversation then and there. Instead, he offered, "It looks to me like they're discouraged, kind of."

"They're a bunch of losers, that's what they are!" Sugar thundered. He yanked open the door to the main hallway and charged through it, leaving Ronde to follow him. "They've got a negative attitude, and Coach Jackson is no better. You'll see soon enough if you haven't already. This is what I live with, and it really, really bites."

Ronde didn't know what to say to that. Clearly, Sugar was upset about the state of the team, and he had every right to be. Everything he'd said was true, technically. What he didn't seem to get was his *own* part in what was wrong with the team.

"Well, there's got to be a way to change things," Ronde said, determined not to give up so easily.

"There's got to be a way to get the front line and the bench involved in playing their best."

He followed Sugar through the main doors and onto the path that led to the parking lot, where the late bus would be waiting for them. "How do you think we could get them to play better?"

Sugar laughed bitterly. "*Me?* How should *I* know? I'm not them."

"Well, who would know better than you?" Ronde wondered. "You've seen every minute of every game from close up. You've been in the locker room, you've won with them and lost with them. You must have some ideas."

Sugar stopped walking, turned to Ronde, and looked right at him. "You're pretty smart, Barber, you know?" he said. "I think having you on the team is gonna make us better. How do you like that, for starters?"

Ronde smiled. "I like it a lot!" he said, and the two of them gave each other five.

"I'm gonna tell Coach to start you," Sugar said, clapping Ronde on the shoulder. "You can't do any worse than Rory's doing. And unlike Tiki, you won't be chucking up shots every time I get you the ball."

"You've got that right," Ronde said. "That's the last thing I want to be doing is shooting. Funny, for a shooting guard, huh?"

He laughed again, but Sugar didn't join in.

In fact, Ronde noticed that he was no longer even

paying attention. Instead, his gaze was fixed on a woman standing by a green car, about halfway to the bus. She was tall and tired-looking, but she was smiling a sad smile and waving to Sean, beckoning him to come over to her.

He looked away from her. "Come on," he said, striding quickly toward the bus. Ronde had to jog to keep up with him.

"What's up?" he asked, but Sugar didn't answer. He walked right by the woman without even looking at her.

"Sean!" she called after him. "Baby, please! Don't be like this. . . ."

Sugar ignored her. He grabbed the door handle and yanked himself up the stairs onto the bus. Ronde paused before following him, and looked back at the woman.

She had put a white handkerchief to her mouth, and her shoulders were heaving up and down. Tears ran down her cheeks. She did not move, but stared after the bus as it rode away.

Ronde sat next to Sugar, but he didn't say a word. He was afraid if he did, Sugar might explode, and all the hard work of making friends with him would go right down the drain.

I might not be able to fix all the basketball team's problems, he thought. *But at least I've finally got a clue about what Sugar's problem might be.*

8

TIKI AT WORK

Tiki had never worked so hard in his life! Hours and hours of packing and unpacking boxes, walking the aisles to take items off shelves and put them on other shelves, then having to write down what he did on two different lists, so that Mr. Landzberg, or his assistant, or his secretary, or his salesmen, could read those lists and know what was where in the warehouse. *Whew!*

Ronde hadn't mentioned *this* part of the job. He'd talked about his errands around downtown Roanoke, and his visits to the house of the boy with the sick mother. But so far, Tiki hadn't left the warehouse even once.

It was kept pretty cold inside too. His floor foreman, Murray Wein, said that a lot of the merchandise kept better that way. But Tiki wondered if it wasn't because it would cost too much to heat a warehouse that size, with such high ceilings. His mom had told the boys their electric bill at home was "outrageous," and you could fit *ten* houses that size in this one big warehouse.

By the time Tiki got home from his first day at work, he was exhausted. And he still had to write his reply to his own "anonymous" letter to the school paper!

Luckily, Ronde wasn't around. "Oh, that's right—he's playing tonight," Tiki remembered aloud.

He looked at the clock over the stove: 7:20 p.m. His mom wasn't home yet either. On Wednesdays, she worked both her jobs.

Seven twenty . . . It wasn't that late at all. Still, it had been dark for over an hour. To Tiki, who was sitting down for the first time since school, it felt like eleven at night.

Still, he sat down to write his advice column. He'd promised it to Laura signed, sealed, and delivered first thing tomorrow morning. He was no welcher, never had been—and he didn't intend to start being one now!

He wrote in his spiral notebook:

Dear "Perplexed,"

Thanks for writing, and I sympathize with your problem. There are lots of kids who act like the one you mention. They don't realize that they're not just hurting themselves, they're hurting everyone in the whole group!

What to do about it? Well, the thing is, as I see it, that this kid—or, let's say, these kinds of kids—need to really look at themselves, and see themselves as others see them. I mean, sure, doing that will really rock their world. But if they're ever going to change, somebody needs to take the risk of laying it all out in the open for them. As the commercial says on TV, "Only your best friend will tell you. . . ."

I hope whoever it is, that they're reading this, and getting the hint. I wish you the courage to speak up to this kid. And I hope if you do, that the kid forgives you, at least after they're done being mad at you for telling it like it is.

Good luck. Your friend, Tiki.

Tiki put down his pen, yawning. He could barely keep his eyes open. The stairs looked a million miles away. He closed his notebook and lay back on the couch . . . just to rest . . . just . . . for a . . . minute . . .

. . .

"TIKI!!"

Tiki shot upright like the spring on a mousetrap. "WHAT?!?"

"Yo, man, come on upstairs and go to bed."

"Wha?"

Aren't I already in bed? Tiki thought, confused. Then he realized he'd dozed off on the living room couch. "What time izzit?"

"Ten o'clock, bro. Time for bed. I've been home for a while, but I let you sleep. You obviously needed it."

"Ah, man . . . work tired me out. . . ."

"I know it," Ronde said. "I didn't say anything about that part, because I didn't want you to feel guilty that I was working all those hours while you were playing b-ball."

Tiki nodded gratefully. "Yeah, thanks for that. Whoa. Everything is sore. . . ." He got up and followed Ronde upstairs.

"Go on, you get washed up first," Ronde said. "I've got to tell you about practice, and what happened after!"

"Aw, man, not tonight," Tiki begged, dragging himself into the bathroom and closing the door behind him. He tried the light switch, but the light blinded him, and he quickly shut it off.

As he brushed his teeth in the dark, he heard Ronde from the other side of the door. "Don't you even want to know?"

"Mphfmgbh," Tiki said, spitting out and rinsing his mouth. He opened the door, and went across the hall to the bedroom with his eyes closed, collapsing onto his bed. "I'm exhausted," he said. "Tell me in the morning."

Over breakfast, Ronde told Tiki about practice, and his conversation with Sugar afterward. Tiki listened intently. "Sounds like you really broke through to the dude," he said approvingly. "I'm glad we switched up, man. You're doing a better job of making friends with him than I ever could. I mean, he can be such a jerk. . . ."

"That's what I thought too," Ronde said, "but then, get this—just when I think I'm getting under his skin, you know? Like we're starting to relate like we're friends? That's when he spots his mom in the parking lot—and suddenly, he froze. It was like I wasn't even there—or worse, like he *wished* I wasn't."

"Weird," Tiki said. "Maybe he and his mom were having a fight or something."

"If they were, it must be pretty bad," said Ronde. "He left her there with the car, and took the bus home."

"Whoa," said Tiki as the bus pulled up to their stop and they got on board. From there all the way to school, they were busy fooling around with their friends, telling jokes and trading gossip.

Sugar Morton was nowhere to be seen, Tiki noticed.

Maybe he and his mom had made up, and she was driving him to school like she used to.

Tiki thought about the advice column he'd written. It was in his book bag, in a sealed envelope, with "for Laura Sommer" written on it.

He'd been pretty harsh on Sugar in his response, he knew. And now he was beginning to regret it. What if Sugar had bigger problems than Tiki knew about? After all, that's what had happened at Landzberg's, where that kid Ralphie had played hooky from work, and everyone was mad at him until Mr. L. sent Ronde to investigate.

Tiki wondered if something similar might be going on in the Morton household. *Maybe I shouldn't print my column*, he thought. *Maybe I should write a new one, with a gentler tone. . . .*

No, there's no time for that, he realized, beginning to panic. Laura would be waiting for him in the entry hall, right by the main office, just like they'd arranged. He couldn't tell her to wait till he'd rewritten the letter. He'd put her off way too long already. Why, oh why, had he ever gotten himself into this mess?

Then he reminded himself of his reason for making up the letter—he wanted Sean Morton to read it, and recognize himself in it! That way, maybe things on the basketball team could begin to change for the better.

Tiki sure hoped it worked. He especially hoped that, whatever happened to the team, his actions wouldn't cause more hurt than people were already feeling.

Laura had had the column for two days already, and Tiki had heard nothing from her. Then, finally, as he was headed for work after Friday classes, he heard her familiar, penetrating voice calling his name from down the hallway.

"Tii-kiii!"

"Oh, hey," he said, waving as she came jogging over to him.

"*Loved* the column!" she gushed. "You are *so good* at this!"

"Uh, thanks . . . I guess," Tiki said, pleased but embarrassed.

"And I hope he gets the message," she went on.

Tiki flinched. "Huh?" He looked around, panicked. Then, satisfied that Sugar was nowhere nearby (of course he wasn't—there was a practice underway in the gym), he turned back to Laura. "Who do you mean?"

"Whomever you're talking about," she said. "Oh, come on, you can tell me. My lips are sealed!"

That was a laugh—Laura's lips were *never* sealed. She was the editor of the school paper, so she always knew whatever was going on. And her job was to print it—or, if she couldn't print it because it was unprintable, to talk about it with everyone she ran into—which was everyone in the school, come to think of it!

"How should I know who the writer was talking about?" Tiki said with a shrug.

"Are you kidding?" she snorted. "I know you wrote that letter!"

"What?!"

"I knew right away—did you think I wouldn't notice? You hand me a letter 'to Tiki' that's written in your own handwriting. Then you turn in your column about it. So I ask myself, 'What's up with that?'" She stared at him, a twinkle of mischief in her eyes. "So, come on, dish—you can tell me—whom are we talking about here?"

"Um . . . I can't really say," said Tiki, his eyes darting this way and that, desperately seeking a way out of this mess he'd gotten himself in. "I was . . . I was sort of sending someone a message."

"Oooooo!! A message!" Laura clapped her hands, delighted with this latest intrigue. "So, let me guess—"

"No!" Tiki stopped her. "No guessing. This column stays confidential, or I'm not doing it anymore."

Ha! He stood there, arms crossed, knowing he had her stymied. She couldn't argue with confidentiality. "So, what do you think?" Tiki asked her. "Will it work?"

"You mean, will he read it?" she asked. "Of course! *Everyone* reads the paper, and everyone reads *your column.*"

"Yeah, but do you think he'll recognize himself?"

"If he does, I hope he doesn't fall apart altogether," Laura said. "That column is pretty hard-hitting."

Just then, Sugar Morton appeared around the corner of the hallway. He went over to his locker, opened it, and took out a basketball. Closing the locker door, he came down the hallway toward them, dribbling the ball as he went. "Hey, Barber! You coming to practice, or what? We're late!"

"No, it's me, Tiki," Tiki said, waving.

"Oh. Sorry," said Sugar, now close enough to see for himself. Since Ronde's haircut, everyone could tell them apart if they looked closely enough.

"Hi, Sean," said Laura.

"Hey, Boo," Sean said, smiling back at her.

"How's it going at home?"

Sean frowned. "Great. Perfect." He kept walking, dribbling the ball a little harder.

"Sorry to hear that," Laura said to his back.

"Don't sweat it. Not your fault. See ya." Tucking the ball under his arm, he pushed open the stairway door and disappeared.

"Poor Sean," she said, sighing, as they both stared at the spot where he'd just been.

"Huh? What do you mean?" Tiki asked, wondering if she knew how frustrated the rest of the team was at Sugar.

"Oh. Well, I guess everyone doesn't know this," she said. "So keep it under your hat. I'm sure Sean doesn't want people talking about his parents' divorce."

"Divorce??"

"I've lived across the street from the Mortons since second grade," Laura said. "His mom left home last month. I haven't seen Sean smile since." She sighed. "Oh, well. Here's hoping it all works out." She patted him on the shoulder and turned to walk away. "Thanks again, Tiki. The column reads like a dream."

"Thanks."

"Sure you don't want to tell me who it's about?"

Tiki smiled and shook his head.

"Oh, well. Paper's out first thing Monday," she called back to him as she went outside.

Tiki stood there, taking it all in. *Divorce!* If only he'd known. That must be why Sugar was acting so hostile toward everyone, and why he was so hard to reach out to!

Tiki felt awful. His column was going to hit the presses, and Sean was probably going to read it. Laura might not have guessed who the column was about, but Sugar would know for sure.

The idea that he might cause any additional pain to Sugar was unbearable. But it was too late to turn back now. Monday morning, the column would be public gossip item number one!

. . .

Ronde was horrified when he heard. "Man," he said, "I wish you'd known that before you wrote that letter!"

"I would never have written it," said Tiki miserably.

"But you know what?" Ronde said. "Maybe it will work out fine."

"Huh?"

"Truth gets out one way or another, sooner or later. And since no one had the guts to tackle it face-to-face with Sugar, maybe this was the only way to move things forward."

"Forward? I hope I didn't just push things off the cliff!"

"Well," said Ronde, "if worse comes to worst, I guess I'll have to be there to pick up the pieces."

9

THE HEART OF THE MATTER

For days, Sugar Morton had barely spoken to Ronde. Ever since they'd been interrupted by the sight of Sugar's mom in the parking lot, it was as if Ronde was getting the silent treatment.

Now, in the visitors' locker room at Blue Ridge Junior High, getting suited up before their crucial game against the Bears, Sugar still kept his distance. He sat deep in thought, staring at his locker, his hands joined between his knees.

"You okay?" Ronde asked him gently.

Sugar turned to him with a bitter expression on his face. "Yeah, man. I'm great. Fantastic. Never been better. Why?"

It was a challenge more than anything. Obviously Sugar was far from fine. What he was really asking Ronde was *Do you want to mess with me?*

Ronde backed off, but Sugar wasn't finished. "Oh, and tell your brother I read his column, and that I'm not stupid."

"He never said you were," Ronde pointed out. "And who says that column is even about you?"

Sugar repeated, "I'm not stupid." And that was all he said. It was game time now, and any further talk would have to wait.

Ronde, too, had to put all questions out of his mind and concentrate on the game. The Eagles really needed this one, after a string of defeats. In fact, they needed to win all their remaining games to finish with a winning record.

That was the goal Coach Jackson had preached to them all week at practice. In all his years of playing organized ball, Ronde had never been on a team with such modest goals. Every team he'd ever been on—even in Pee-Wee League football—had made the play-offs at the very least!

Suddenly, Ronde could feel the sting of it. He knew it was just a taste of how he would feel if this team didn't finish above .500.

Coach came up to Ronde and pulled him aside. "I'm not starting you," he said, "even though I'd like to. You and Sugar won us the game last week."

"Me and . . . ?" Ronde couldn't believe his ears.

"You play great defense, Ronde. Besides, Sugar

seems to like you—or at least, he likes playing with you."

Ronde nodded. Coach Jackson obviously hadn't heard the exchange he'd just had with Sugar.

"It's just . . . I just can't do that to Rory," the coach finished. "You understand? He's been the starter ever since Brian Reynolds left for military school. It would kill whatever's left of his confidence."

"Totally," Ronde said. "I'm down with that." He'd been in Rory's position too, and he knew what getting benched felt like.

"But be ready," Coach Jackson said, squeezing Ronde's shoulder. "You won't be sitting long. We've got to win this game. When you get your chance, you have to be ready and run with it."

Well, thought Ronde. *That much is good, at least.* The coach was acting like he cared, like he wanted victory with all his heart. And that, as Ronde well knew, was how you built a winning team.

Ronde watched as the game began. Bobby Dominic was getting pushed around by the Bears' center under the basket. He kept yelling for the officials to call a foul, but Ronde could tell that Rory was just too skinny and weak to hold off the pressure of the big players Blue Ridge had up front.

Rory was having trouble getting free. The Bears' shooting guard was on him every step of the way. Ronde thought he looked familiar. Then he realized he'd seen the kid before—under a football helmet! So, he and Tiki weren't the only athletes to think of playing multiple sports! Ronde shook his head and smiled.

Sugar, of course, was at the heart of it all, as usual. He did most of the ball-handling. Whenever the Bears double-teamed him, causing him to stop dribbling, he would pass it to one of the Eagles' forwards, Larry Budnick or Jake Lewis. He never went to Rory Mathis because Rory was being covered like a blanket by his counterpart on the Bears. As for Bobby Dominic, he was being pushed around like a broomstick.

When Larry or Jake got a pass from Sugar, they would just pass it right back to him. It was Sugar doing all the shooting. And right now, he was ice cold.

By the time Coach Jackson called his first time-out, the Eagles were already desperate. The score was 14–5, Bears.

"Ronde, you're in for Rory," Jackson said. Rory nodded, seemingly relieved to be sitting down.

"That guy is super-tough to guard," he told Ronde. "And he sticks to you like flypaper. I wish you luck."

"You've got to put him to sleep, dude," Ronde said. "Watch me. I'll show you."

Out on the court, Ronde seemed suddenly lazy. He seemed to be just standing there. Then, just as he sensed the defender relaxing his guard, he made his move.

"Hit me!" he yelled to Sugar, who was desperately fighting off the double-team.

Sugar saw that Ronde was free and heading for the basket—but instead of passing, he made a move of his own. He crashed into the two kids guarding him, and the ref blew his whistle.

"That's a charge!" the ref yelled, pointing to Sugar. "Bears' ball!"

"What??" Sugar yelled, stamping his feet. "That's garbage!"

The ref blew his whistle and pointed to Sugar. "And that's a technical! One more word out of you, and you're out of the game, understand?"

Sugar opened his mouth to answer, but Coach Jackson stopped him by pulling him gently away. "Hey!" he barked into Sugar's ear. "We need you on the court! You can't go getting yourself thrown out of games!"

Sugar nodded, still eyeing the official. He went to the bench and sat down, and seventh grader Dave Bassin, who almost never got much game time because he was Sugar's backup at point guard, came in as his replacement.

Ronde covered his man perfectly as the Bears inbounded after their free throws. He kept his focus on his man's midsection, not his eyes. Ronde knew the way good broken-field runners use their eyes to fool the defender.

Well, he wasn't biting. The Bears turned it over. It was the first break the Eagles had gotten all game.

On offense, though, there was utter confusion. Without Sugar there to dominate control of the ball, everyone was suddenly calling for it! Even if they were only the least bit free, their hands went up, vying for Dave's attention.

He turned from one to the next, and in doing so, took his eyes off the defender. Before he knew it, the ball had been knocked away!

Ronde saw it coming, and was on it before anyone else could get there. He looked up—and there was Bobby under the basket, alone! Ronde whipped a pass to him, and Bobby threw up an easy layup for the score!

The home crowd erupted in cheers. It wasn't often the Eagles cashed in without Sugar on the court.

Ronde took a quick look over at the Eagle bench, and saw Sugar arguing with Coach Jackson. *He wants back in,* he said to himself. He wondered how long Coach J. would leave his star on the bench with a crucial game on the line.

As long as we keep it close, he told himself, *Coach won't make a substitution.* He was determined that he and the others now on the court were going to put on a show.

Ronde darted forward and snagged another loose ball. He dribbled quickly down the court—never mind that he wasn't the point guard, he was free!

He could hear a defender closing on him from behind, and pulled up short. The defender hit him like a two-ton truck. Ronde went down, and the whistle blew.

"Foul!" yelled the ref.

Ronde got up and checked himself for bruises. *Not too bad,* he judged. Standing at the free throw line, he took the ball and calmly sank one shot, then another.

Sugar wound up sitting the whole rest of the first half. When the buzzer sounded, the Eagles were in the lead, 32–28. Ronde had scored seven points, five of them on free throws. He'd notched three rebounds, three steals, and two assists. It was the best performance by an Eagle not named Sugar in anyone's memory!

Ronde felt really, really good. He was proud of what he'd done, and even though his teammates slapped him five, and he knew they were as excited as he was, none of them said much, other than "nice going."

In the locker room at halftime, he wondered whether Sugar would say *anything* to him. Before the game, he'd been really angry with Tiki, and with Ronde, too. Would Ronde's great work on the court change Sugar's attitude for the better?

Or *worse*?

Here came Sugar now. He looked straight at Ronde and said, "Way to go."

Ronde breathed a sigh of relief. "Thanks!"

"Coach is pairing us up for the second half. That means you're in for the start."

"Oh." Ronde paused. "But . . . what about Rory?"

"You're in," Sugar said simply. That was all he said, except, "See you out there. You know what to do with the ball when you get it, right?"

Ronde nodded. He knew what Sugar expected him to do—pass it straight to Sugar.

He glanced over at Rory, who was sitting glumly in front of his locker. Ronde got up and went over there. "Don't worry, man," he said, sitting next to him on the bench. "I'm gonna fix this whole mess."

"Yeah, you fixed it great so far," said Rory, not looking at him.

Ronde got up without saying anything more. Rory was bound to be mad at him for taking his place on the starting five. That was natural. But Ronde had meant what he'd said: He meant to fix this mess, and soon.

The second half was a pitched battle, between the Bears on one side and Ronde and Sugar on the other.

In a way, Ronde had succeeded—he'd convinced Sugar to share the ball, the way a good point guard should. The bad part was, the only one he'd share the ball with was Ronde. And he was doing that only because he knew Ronde would pass it right back to him!

On the *other* hand, Ronde did find himself free for

a few easy shots—and when he did, he sank them. Sugar did his part, dazzling the Bears' defense with his moves and his soft-touch jumpers, passing off to Ronde whenever the Bears came at him with the double-team.

"That's what I'm talkin' about!" Sugar roared when the Blue Ridge coach had to call an emergency time-out to keep the Eagles from running away with the game. "That's what I've been trying to get going all season!"

Yeah, Ronde said silently to himself. *Now try it with everybody else on the team!*

He said nothing out loud, of course. Not now, in the middle of a crucial ball game. But Ronde knew he'd have to say something soon—this team needed every victory it could get. One more loss, and it would mean the end of their last remaining goal: a winning season.

For today, Ronde and Sugar's heroics were enough. The Eagles won by a score of 57–54. Sugar scored only seventeen points, but Ronde's eleven points helped to make up the difference.

Okay, so they'd kept their dream alive, he thought as he followed the team back into the locker room—for today, at least. But that was small comfort. The Bears were a losing team, well below the Eagles in the standings.

Both of the Eagles' remaining games were against play-off contenders, and the Eagles needed to win out in order to finish over .500. One thing was for sure—they were going to need more than two effective players to do it.

Ronde knew that if things were going to shift, today had to be the day. Now had to be the time.

He wasn't sure how to start the conversation. But luckily, Sugar helped him out by starting it himself.

"Yo, Ronde," he said, waving him over to his locker. "You ready to get out of here?"

"Uh, yeah," Ronde said, nodding. "Got all my stuff. Sure, I'm ready."

"Let's go." He led the way, and Ronde followed. Most of their teammates had already showered, changed, and left for home. "The bus'll be waiting."

Rory Mathis was still sitting by his locker, in full uniform. He stared after Ronde as he and Sugar left, and Ronde wondered what he was thinking.

There were others on the bus, and they all wanted to high-five Sugar and Ronde. Ronde obliged, but he couldn't get the image of Rory out of his mind. He'd taken over the poor kid's spot—and it wasn't the coach who'd made the switch, it was Sugar! *That would surely never have happened on the football team,* he knew. Now, Rory probably thought Ronde had made friends with Sugar just so he could take over as starter.

Sugar sat down on the bus, and saved the seat next to him for Ronde. Soon they were on their way back to

Hidden Valley, and the roar of the bus's engine made it easy for the two boys to talk without kids in the nearby rows hearing them.

"Sorry about chewing you out before the game," Sugar said. "I know you're not your brother."

"My brother's the best there is," Ronde said, sticking up for Tiki.

He meant it too. Sugar saw, and backed down.

"Sure, sure," he said. "Whatever. But that column he wrote was just sour grapes, yo. He was a shooting guard who couldn't shoot straight, you know?"

"He shoots fine," Ronde said pointedly, "when people don't get all over his back about it. He doesn't need that extra pressure—he puts enough pressure on himself."

Sugar shrugged, and sighed. "Okay, okay. He sure is great at football, anyway. You are too—but you can also play some awesome defense. Tonight was pure, man. That was a show you put on. How many steals?"

"I don't know . . . seven . . ."

"That's right. You do know. And you should be proud of yourself, dude. You got your chance, and you ran with it."

"Thanks . . . I guess . . ."

"You've got to be a little selfish in this world, you know?" Sugar went on, as if they were suddenly best friends, sharing their innermost thoughts. "In the end, everybody's all about 'me.' It's crazy not to be the same, and even more so."

"Is *that* what you think?" Ronde asked. *"Really?"*

"Sure," Sugar said, taken aback. "Why not? My mom walked out on the rest of us, did you know that?"

Ronde caught his breath. Should he admit that he did know? For a moment, he considered playing innocent—but then, he figured it was best to just be as up-front as possible. Sugar obviously felt betrayed enough as it was. "Um . . . I . . ."

Sugar didn't wait for his answer. "That's right—one day, out of nowhere, she just up and drove away. She left a note saying it wasn't because of me or my sister, that we were great kids, blah, blah, blah." He snorted. "It was all about *her*, see? And now I realize, that's how it is with *everybody*."

Ronde thought about that statement for a moment. "I don't believe that," he finally said. "I don't think it's that way, not for most people."

Sugar frowned. "You're just a sucker, Barber. Watch out somebody doesn't let you down big-time."

"What about your dad?" Ronde asked. "Where was he during all this?"

Sugar's jaw grew tense as he stared at the seat back in front of him. "My dad works a lot . . . travels a lot . . . but at least he was there for us when he was home."

Ronde thought he saw Sugar's chin quiver for a split

second, but then it set itself tight again. "Nobody was thinking about me or my sister. My parents would be fighting all the time, and nobody bothered to come say good night to us."

Ronde felt for him. It was painful just to be sitting this close to someone who was so hurt and angry. And worst of all, Ronde knew it was up to him to say the right thing—the one thing that would change Sugar's way of thinking about other people.

The bus was getting close to his stop. There wasn't much time left. What could he say . . . ? What *should* he say . . . ?

"You say your dad is always there for you when you need him. But your mom was there in the parking lot that night last week, and you wouldn't even *look* at her."

He knew he'd taken a risk by saying it out loud. That moment had obviously been upsetting to Sugar. He'd shut Ronde out from then right up until now. But somehow, Ronde felt sure that this was at the bottom of Sugar's problem, and unless they could talk about it, there was no further progress to be made. That made it a risk worth taking.

Sugar had reacted badly that night in the parking lot, and this time was no different. "You think you know all about it, huh, Barber?" he said bitterly. "You don't know *anything. Nothing,* you hear? Nothing!!"

. . .

"And that was it," Ronde finished telling Tiki as they sat up in their beds that night. "Everyone on the bus knew he was mad, and they all asked me what was up, but I didn't say anything. Luckily, it was my stop, so I didn't have to hang around."

Tiki shook his head. "That's got to be it, Ronde! This business with his parents' divorce has got him all messed up, and he's taking it out on everybody else—including the team!"

"Man, we are going to *lose* these games coming up unless something changes," Ronde said, defeated. "I've done what I can do, Tiki. He totally shut me out."

Tiki stared up at the glow-in-the-dark stars that shone down at them from the ceiling, green in the darkness. "We've got some time till next game," he said. "I've got one more thing I want to try before then."

10

A PIECE OF ADVICE

"I've got another column I want to write," Tiki told Laura.

"Is this in answer to *another* letter you wrote yourself?" she asked with a crooked grin.

He handed her the letter—typed this time—signed *"Crushed."*

She read it out loud. *"Dear Tiki, I am doing a group project with someone whose parents just got divorced, and he's all upset about it. That would be bad enough, but what's worse is, he's making life miserable for everyone around him. This group project is the most important thing a lot of us have ever been involved in, and he's ruining it for us. If he doesn't stop it soon, it will be too late, and the whole project will be a failure. What should I tell him? Sincerely, 'Crushed.'"* Laura squinted, then looked up at Tiki. "Honestly. *'Crushed'*?"

JUMP SHOT

"Hey, that's the name they used."

"I don't know," Laura said. "It's a little too much like the last one. Different, but the same in a kind of way, if you know what I mean. I've got a pile of others you can pick from."

"Listen," Tiki said, "you liked my column last time, didn't you?"

"Of course I did!" she said, smiling.

"So, then trust me, okay?" he said. "This one will be even better."

"Not that I *really* trust you, but go ahead," she said with a shrug. "What do I care so long as it reads well. But come on, Tiki—you can be honest with me—this is about the same kid, right? Same as the last letter—what was it . . . ? *'Perplexed'*?"

"What makes you say that?"

"Come on," she said. "First of all, there's all this talk about a group, and a project, and a kid acting badly."

"So? That could be a coincidence!" Tiki sighed. "Anyway, what do you care?"

"I don't—but come on, you can tell me. It is the same kid, isn't it?"

"Okay, yes, yes it is. Now can I leave? I've got to get to my job at the warehouse."

"Okay, okay, wait, wait, don't tell me . . . this is Kevin O'Hara, isn't it?"

"Who?"

"Oh, come on, I wasn't born yesterday," said Laura, pleased with herself. She waved a hand at him. "You can't fool me. It's all about 'the group.' Kevin's the lead in the play, his parents are getting divorced, and I hear he's been a real pain to work with."

"Uh . . . I can't say if it's him or not," said Tiki, glad she was off on the wrong trail. For a minute there, he was sure she'd guessed who the columns were really about!

"Don't worry," she said, "my lips are sealed. ZZZZZZIP!" She pretended to zip her lips shut, but Tiki knew that Laura would soon share her "secret" with at least a dozen other people, all of whom would then share it with their closest friends, who of course would never tell a soul. Soon, the whole school would know.

Except they'd be wrong.

Oh, well—poor Kevin. Tiki barely knew the kid, but he didn't feel too badly. After all, it was Laura, not him, who'd said it was Kevin. He had neither confirmed nor denied, and she'd drawn her own conclusions.

To Tiki, the most important thing was that Sugar's identity remained secret.

"You know, divorce doesn't have to be the worst thing in the world," Laura went on, just as Tiki was about to grab his book bag and get out of there. "Sometimes, it's even a good thing."

"Huh?" He turned back around to face her. "I don't get it. How's that possible?"

"Well, just for instance," she said, "*my* parents broke up a long time ago—and *thank goodness!*"

"*What?!*"

Laura waved her hand dismissively, as if it were the most natural thing in the world. "They *never* got along," she said. "Always screaming at each other, *and* at me . . . things are much better now. Quieter, and everyone gets along. I see my dad twice a month, and it's always very cool. We have fun. He and my mom are even nicer to each other now that they don't live together. Nobody fights, and I still feel like I have both my parents."

Tiki nodded slowly. "You know," he told Laura, "I think you just gave me the hook for my column. Thanks!" He grabbed his book bag. "Gotta run—can't be late for work!"

"She said it was actually good that it happened!" Tiki exclaimed.

"Wow," Ronde said, before stuffing another whole ravioli into his mouth. "Mphfgm."

"So I'm thinking, I'm going to write another column, just for Sugar, all about making the best of a bad situation, for the good of the family and the team. The paper comes out on Friday. That's the day of the next game, so your job is to get him to read it before he goes out on the court."

"I don't know," Ronde said. "He may not even be talking to me anymore."

"Come on," Tiki said. "You've got practice tomorrow. Tell him you're sorry you stuck your nose in his business. He'll forgive you."

"I'm not so sure. He's pretty ticked off at the world right now, let alone me."

"You know, other people have problems besides Sugar," Tiki said. "Look at Ralphie. He's got even worse problems! And he *never* gets mad, or treats anyone like dirt."

"It's different," Ronde said. "Sugar's a *star. Everyone* knows him and wants to be his friend."

"Except the kids on the team," Tiki pointed out. "They've all had it with him."

"I know," said Ronde. "That's what I'm afraid of. We need them to get their heads in the game and contribute to the team!"

"Just make sure he reads my column," Tiki said. "If anything will change Sugar's mind now, it's what I'm going to write."

"If you say so," Ronde said. "I just hope it's not too late."

11

PUSH COMES TO SHOVE

Something was wrong. Ronde could tell right away. Usually, when he entered the locker room, there was a buzz of conversation, along with some laughter. Today, it was dead silent. Kids were looking at one another with wide, anxious eyes.

"Man, you just missed it," Rory said as Ronde looked his way.

"What? What'd I miss?"

"The fight of the century," said Bobby Dominic. "Sugar went ape on Dave Bassin."

"WHAT?"

"Dave's on his way to the nurse's office, and Sugar's with the dean," Rory explained. "He hit him right in the eye."

"Whoa," said Ronde, sinking down onto the bench in front of his locker. "What happened? Who started it?"

"I was standing right there when it happened," said Larry Budnick, the team's starting power forward. "Dave said something about what a brat Sugar was being, and how his parents must have been sleeping on the job bringing him up—and suddenly, with, like, no warning, Sugar went off on him. Before Bassin even knew what hit him, he'd taken a punch in the eye, and Sugar was looking for more."

"Rory and I were barely able to hold him back," Bobby confirmed.

"Where was Coach all this time?" Ronde wondered aloud.

"He separated them as quick as he could," said Larry. "But Dave had a bloody nose, and he said he was seeing blurry, so . . ."

"Man, that is *baaad* news," Ronde said, shaking his head. He couldn't see any way now for the team to come together.

Yet as bad as things were, they were about to get even worse.

Coach Jackson came into the locker room looking stern and worried. They all gathered around him, clamoring to hear the latest news. "Sugar's suspended for three days," said the coach. "He's lucky he wasn't thrown off the team altogether, if you ask me."

Ronde nodded. If it had been any other player, he *would* have been off the team, no doubt about it. But the Eagles were built around Sugar and his talent. If he were taken off the team, the rest of the season would surely go right down the drain.

"How's Dave?" Ronde asked.

Coach Jackson shook his head. "Better, but still seeing a little blurry out of that one eye. He'll have to miss this week's game too."

A moan went up from the players. "What are we going to do?" Bobby said. "Bassin was Sugar's backup. Now we don't have a single point guard on our roster!"

"Yes we do," said the coach, and he looked right at Ronde. "You may not be much of a shooter, kid, but you can handle the ball as well as anybody—and you're a good passer, too."

Ronde felt pleased to be singled out for praise, but he knew it was also a heavy responsibility, stepping in for a talent like Sugar Morton.

"So if Ronde's moving over to point, who's our second shooting guard?" Rory wondered. "And who's going to back him up at point?"

The lightbulb went off in all their minds at the same time. "Tiki!" the shout went up.

"Oh, wait a minute, I don't know," Ronde warned. "He's pretty busy with his job and the school paper. . . ."

But even as he said it, he knew his twin would find a way somehow. If there was a team that needed him, there was nothing in this world that could keep Tiki Barber from answering the call.

For Ronde, it was an exciting prospect. No matter how bad the news was about Sugar and Dave, no matter how much of a challenge it presented for the rest of the team—for the Barber boys, this would be a signature moment.

The two of them, out on the court together, part of their school basketball team!

Ronde knew it would be tough. He had never led a basketball team before, except in his wildest dreams, fooling around in the driveway by himself or with Tiki, and sometimes with Paco and their other friends from the neighborhood. Ronde or Tiki would offer up a play-by-play featuring their pretend heroics. It was fun— and only that.

This would be the real deal.

Ronde floated through practice, almost as if he were playing the part of the star point guard in a movie about the Hidden Valley Eagles.

He could feel the rest of the team come alive around him too. Bobby, Rory, Larry—everyone who'd basically been standing around all season while Sugar lit up the scoreboard. Suddenly, even though it was only practice, they were playing with passion and excitement!

They all knew this next game would be their big

chance to prove themselves, to show everyone what a team without a star can accomplish, to take those key shots with the clock winding down, and to notch a historic victory for their school and their team.

"That was awesome!" Rory said between panting breaths as they got back to the locker room after practice.

"Best we've ever played," Bobby agreed breathlessly. "Too bad it wasn't a real game."

"We've got to carry this forward," Ronde urged. "This is who we are, guys. We are *for real*. Like my mama says, we've got to go out there and *play proud!*"

"PLAY PROUD!!" they all repeated, over and over again, and the chant was so loud, it made the lockers shake.

"Me? Really?"

Ronde could see that Tiki was as excited as he was at the thought of rejoining the team.

"I mean, that stinks about Sugar," Tiki said. "And especially about Dave Bassin."

"The doctor said his eye will be okay in a few days," Ronde assured him. "And as for Sugar . . . well, I feel bad for him, but maybe this is what will finally wake him up."

"I've got something else that might wake him up,"

Tiki said, fishing out a big envelope. "Or at least, give him reason to hope."

"Your column?"

"Uh-huh. It'll be out in the school paper tomorrow afternoon."

Ronde took it and read it through. He quickly saw that Tiki had taken care with every word.

Dear "Crushed,"

I know how frustrating it must be to see your whole group suffer on account of one person's suffering. But the only way to save the situation is to be honest with him (or her). Tell him that divorce is tough on kids, but that a whole lot of kids go through it, and it's probably no easier for them.

Also, a lot of times, things can be fine after a split, once everybody gets their own act together. If everyone can stay friendly, he might get to see a lot of both his parents. And his parents might be happier than before (nothing like having happy parents!).

Tell him to hang in there and be patient with both

his parents. They're probably having a tough time too. And tell him to remember—in the end, things may still turn out really well, as long as everyone treats everyone else with love and respect.

Tell him your group project is also important, and that the rest of you in the group are like a temporary family. Taking his troubles out on the rest of you is just dooming that family to failure.

Tell him to try to set his own troubles aside, at least while he's with the group. And tell him you care about him, too. That's what makes the difference in the end—people caring about one another.

All the best, and good luck. Your friend, Tiki.

"This is great," Ronde said. "I'm going to make sure Sugar gets to see it."

"How're you going to do that?" Tiki asked. "He's suspended for three days, right?"

"This can't wait," Ronde said firmly. "Leave it to me." He glanced at the envelope again.

"Don't worry," Tiki assured him. "It can't hurt him any worse than he's already hurt himself. And it might just help him turn this funk of his around."

Ronde nodded. He put the column back in its envelope. "You got a copy?"

Tiki nodded. Then he took a breath and blew it out. "Hey, Ronde?"

"Yeah?"

"You really think I can do this?"

"What do you mean?" Ronde said. Then he realized. "Oh. The game."

Tiki nodded.

"You already finished your column, right? And I'm sure Mr. Landzberg will give you the day off if you tell him it's an emergency."

Tiki furrowed his brow. "It *is* an emergency, kind of . . . isn't it?"

"*Sure* it is!" Ronde replied eagerly. "If you don't come through for us, this team will never see .500!"

Tiki frowned. "I don't know," he said. "I guess I can get permission all right. . . . But what if I wind up messing up? I mean, I've barely had any time with the team—just a couple weeks really, and that was over a month ago. What if I'm rusty? What if my shot's gone south?"

"Come on, bro," Ronde said, grinning. "You know you've still got that mojo working. You *know* you *want* this!"

"Sure I want it," Tiki said. "But really . . . what if my shot isn't there? I haven't been to a single practice lately. You're part of the team now, but I haven't even had time to shoot in the driveway!"

"That doesn't matter," Ronde told him. "Remember, you're coming off the bench for both me and Rory. If you're doing better at point guard, you'll play more there. If you're the hot hand at shooting, that's where you'll be. And bro—think of it—you and me, out on the basketball court—together! It's meant to be, right?"

Tiki grinned from ear to ear. "You got that right," he said, and they exchanged their private handshake—twice!

"Besides," Ronde said, growing more serious, "it's not your soft-touch jump shot we need most. And it's not how we play point guard—the whole team knows neither of us has ever played there."

"Then what is it? Our defense?" Tiki asked.

"It's that we both know how to *lead a team*," Ronde said. "These guys wouldn't follow Sugar, because he never tried to lead them—he went off on his own without them! We're going to lead our team into battle, Tiki, and they're going to follow us, because they know we *care* about them."

"What are you doing here?" Sugar's breath came out in a cloud as he stood in the doorway of his family's house on Exeter Street. "Jeez, it's cold out there," he said. "Come on in and let me close the door."

Ronde entered the house and looked around. He'd never been to Sugar's before, even though it was only five blocks from Amherst Street, where the Barbers lived. The place was quiet—a grandfather clock ticked slowly in the hallway, and the carpeted floors muffled any sounds—but Ronde didn't think anyone else was home.

"What are you doing here, Ronde?" Sugar wanted to know. "It's freezing cold out there."

It was dark, too, though Sugar hadn't mentioned that part. Ronde had biked over here, and nearly frozen his ears off, even though he had on a stocking cap.

"I came to deliver the paper," Ronde said. Reaching into his pocket, he pulled out a rolled-up, rubber-banded paper, and tossed it to Sugar.

Sugar let it drop on the floor in front of him. "I'm not reading any more of your brother's stupid columns," he said. "Thanks for stopping by." He moved to open the door and let Ronde out, but Ronde's hand stopped him.

"I've got something to say first," he told Sugar.

"Who says I want to hear it?"

"*I* do. You going to punch me in the eye too?"

Sugar's jaw tensed, but he kept his temper under control. "He deserved it."

"Nuh-uh," Ronde insisted. "Nobody deserves to get punched. That's why people invented words, yo."

Sugar frowned, but said nothing.

"And speaking of words, I've got a few choice ones for you. I've been meaning to say this ever since I got on the team, but—well, I don't know if you've noticed, but your attitude has infected the whole team."

"What?!"

"That's right. The way you get your game on is hurting everybody *else's* game."

Sugar snorted. "You don't know what you're talking about."

Ronde ignored the insult. "The thing I want to know is, what's really eating you?"

"Eating me? Nothing. I'm fine," Sugar insisted.

"Dude, trust me, you are not fine. You are the furthest thing from fine. I mean, maybe you can't see it the way other people can, but you're angry *all the time.*"

"I am not!" Sugar said angrily. Then he realized that his tone was making him a liar. "I mean, I guess I am sometimes. Who isn't?"

"You're angry not just *some* of the time," Ronde said frankly. "I think you're sad, too. And maybe a little bitter?"

Sugar laughed bitterly. "Ya think?" he said. "Like I haven't got anything to be bitter about. . . ."

"Go on," Ronde said. "Let's hear it."

"Why should I tell *you* about it?"

"Because," said Ronde, "it's destroying the team, dude."

"Ha!" said Sugar. "That's a good one. I'm the best player on that team by far!"

"True, but the way you've been acting is making you the *only* player on the team. Ever notice how much the rest of the guys wind up just standing around on the court?"

"It's hard *not* to notice," Sugar had to admit. "Those guys don't really care whether we win or lose."

"You're wrong, man," Ronde said. "They may not care *now*, but they *used* to care. And they *could* care *again*—if they felt they were part of the team."

"I don't get you," said Sugar. "What are you asking me to do? I play my heart out every single game!"

"I know you do," said Ronde. "That's why we've still got a chance to have a winning season! But now you've gone and gotten yourself suspended from school, and we've got to play our next game without you. And why? Because you let your angry, sad, bitter feelings get the better of you. Now Dave Bassin has a black eye, and we've got to win without our best player *and* his substitute! What good did you think you were doing the team by punching him out like that?"

"He said something about my parents," Sugar said, staring into space, angered by even the memory of it.

"Okay, he shouldn't have done that," Ronde agreed. "But you didn't have to deal with it the way you did."

Sugar sighed. "I guess you're right about that. I

kind of lost control. I couldn't help myself."

"Let me tell you something," said Ronde. "I was on the football team for three whole years. I know you get angry sometimes when things get tough. But you've got to think about the whole team, not just yourself."

"You just don't understand," Sugar said, sighing. "My life this year has been . . ." He stopped talking, and Ronde could see that he was fighting back tears.

"Hey, man," Ronde said, his tone softening, "I know it's been tough on you."

"You have no idea," said Sugar. "My whole family's breaking apart." He sniffed once, then again. The silence in the house was deafening.

"My dad works all the time," he finally went on. "My mom? She didn't care enough about me and my sister to stick around and work it out. Nobody cares about us kids . . . so I decided I had to look after myself. Nobody is going to help *me* out, and nobody is going to feel sorry for me—so *I've* got to make sure I get what I need."

"Wow," said Ronde. "You should hear yourself."

"What do you mean?"

"You sound so . . . so *selfish.*"

"*Me?* What about my mom? My dad? You think they're not being selfish?" He laughed again, with that same bitter note. "You don't know a thing about it. I'm alone here, on my own. My sister's only ten, and she's crying all the time." Ronde looked around, and Sugar explained, "She's sleeping over at a friend's house."

"Listen," Ronde said, "I hear you, and I *do* understand. Maybe you think my life and Tiki's is a bed of roses."

"It isn't?"

"No! Did you know my mom has raised us all by herself, all these years? She works all the time, too, just like your dad—except she works *two* jobs, not one, and I'll bet she doesn't make half as much money as he does." Ronde could tell that just by looking at the expensive furniture in Sugar's house.

"My brother and I have to work at an after-school job, and give all the money we make to our mom so she can pay the bills," he went on. "It's just me and Tiki, eating dinner alone half the time. But you don't see *us* complaining. We take what life gives us, and we make the best of it!"

Sugar was silent, taking it all in.

"We know our mom loves us, with all her heart. So we do our best to help her, however we can—washing dishes, mowing the lawn, contributing money from our job—whatever it takes. We're a *family*, and we stick *together*. You and your sister and your dad, you need to do that too, now that your mom's not around."

Ronde winced, wishing he hadn't said that. "I mean, like you told me, at least he's there for you."

"When he's here," Sugar said.

"Same with my mom. Sometimes parents have to work, so their kids will have food and clothes and a roof over their heads."

"At least your mom loves you," Sugar said. "My mom couldn't care less about us."

"I'm sure that's not true," Ronde said.

"She left us, just like that. No good-bye, no nothing. Not even a note. If she loved us, she would have said something."

"Maybe she had her reasons, that had nothing to do with you," Ronde guessed. "Anyway, if she doesn't love you, why was she there waiting for you in the parking lot that night?"

Sugar shifted uncomfortably on the stair where he'd sat down. He stared at the floor.

"She was crying, did you notice? Did you even give her a chance to explain?"

When Sugar didn't answer, Ronde kept talking. "You know, sometimes it's even worse for kids if their parents are always fighting and yelling and screaming, and they just can't get along. Sometimes it's best if people separate."

"It's not best for me and my sister!" Sugar said, his jaw tight. "Nobody's thinking about what's best for us."

"Well, hey," said Ronde, not backing down, "then you, better than anyone, should know to think about the rest of your teammates. We're kind of like a family too, right? How do you think the guys feel when you dump all over them?"

Ronde opened the door to leave, and let Sugar think about what he'd said. Then he pointed to the paper lying at the foot of the stairs. "Oh, by the way. You really should read Tiki's advice column this week. You might learn something."

12

ALL IN THE FAMILY

Tiki had suffered through his classes all day. He couldn't keep his mind from wandering. Fantasies of glory on the court alternated with nightmares where he blew the game for the team. Twice, teachers had called his name in vain, causing his classmates to laugh when he finally realized what was going on.

The only good parts of the day came when he ran into his teammates in the hall or at lunch. Every one of them seemed excited that he was going to be playing with them that afternoon. He was glad to be welcomed— he just hoped he wouldn't let them down in their hour of need.

Today's game was a real challenge. With two games left to play in their season, the Eagles were 7–8. Both their remaining opponents had winning records. Today's game was against the North Side Rockets, who were in first place in the league, with a 13–2 record. What made it even harder was that the Eagles were the visiting team. At home, the Rockets were undefeated, at 7–0.

The rest of the team didn't seem all that worried about it, though. On the bus, and in the visitors' locker room, everyone seemed full of energy and good spirits. Tiki wondered why, until Ronde clued him in. "They're into playing, because they know that today, it's up to them, not Sugar."

Tiki understood then, and smiled. He only hoped Sugar had read his column. Ronde didn't seem to think he would read it, but what else could either of them do to get through to the team's troubled superstar?

For now, there was only one mission, though, and Sugar had nothing to do with it. That mission was to win, and Tiki meant to accomplish it, no matter what.

This part was familiar to him. The football Eagles had had their backs to the wall many times, and they'd always found a way to win when it mattered most.

Coach Jackson laid out the game plan. "Ronde will start at point, with Rory at shooting guard. Budnick and Jarvis start at forward, and Bobby at center. Tiki will be first man off the bench, subbing for both Rory and Ronde. Got it?"

They all clapped their hands, and Tiki could see the light of determination in all their eyes. This, he thought, was going to be interesting. . . .

The first thing he noticed when he entered the gym was the size of the Rockets. They were much bigger than the Eagles—taller, wider, thicker, and heavier. They had bulging muscles and an air of confidence that was impossible to miss. Probably because, Tiki thought, the last time these two teams had met, the Rockets had handled the Eagles easily, 72–57.

They would also have noticed that Sugar Morton was missing. Well, thought Tiki, if ever a team was ripe for a fall, it was the Rockets. The way he figured it, the Eagles had them right where they wanted them. The Rockets were in for a nasty surprise.

The game began, and Tiki cheered from the bench as the Eagles put on a clinic in passing and defense. Almost every time down the court, everyone on the team touched the ball at least once. Tiki was sure that had never happened with Sugar at the point guard position.

On defense, the Eagles were all over the ball-carrier. Bobby was holding his own against a much bigger center for the Rockets. And Ronde kept finding Rory in the open, where he sank his first four shots in a row.

By the time Tiki got in the game, and Ronde sat down, the Eagles were up by six points, and the crowd in the North Side gym was beginning to get restless. Tiki started right in by stealing the inbounds pass, then chucking it upcourt to Rory, who laid it in for the score!

Quickly, Tiki got back on D. Just in time, too. The

Rockets' shooting guard nearly bowled him over, but Tiki had established position, and the ref called the other kid for a charging foul.

Tiki took the ball downcourt. He looked for Rory, but could see that he was gassed. Rory was breathing heavily, his hands on his hips. Instead, Tiki found Bobby under the basket, and he sank the shot with a foul on top of it.

Coach Jackson sent Ronde back in and called Rory to the bench. Tiki beamed. For the first time in any sport, he and his twin were in a game at the same time, on the same team! Tiki was now the shooting guard, with Ronde taking over at the point.

Each time up the court on offense, Tiki would put on one of the patented moves he'd perfected on the football field. Ronde, who knew him better than anyone, would pass the ball to him in stride, timing it perfectly so that Tiki could get the shot off cleanly. The Eagles went on another run, and by the time Tiki sat down again, they were up by twelve points!

"This is even better than in the driveway!" Tiki yelled to his brother after one play, and Ronde nodded back, laughing.

North Side called another time-out. Tiki high-fived the entire bench, including Rory, who said as he was going back in, "This is the best we've played all year—thanks to you two guys!"

Tiki was pleased, but a little embarrassed. He knew Sugar Morton was a much better basketball player than either him or Ronde. But sometimes, he knew, it mattered more how well your teammates played *around* you.

Today, they were playing with fire and passion, and the Rockets were in full panic mode. Oh, they'd be making it to the play-offs, whatever happened today, Tiki knew. Still, the shame of losing to a much weaker team was not pleasant, especially if you were in first place and thought of yourselves as the best in the league.

At halftime, the Eagles held an eight-point lead. Ronde and Tiki had tired at the same time, and there was no other substitute at guard. The Rockets had taken advantage with a little run of their own in the final two minutes, to make the score respectably close and give themselves a fighting chance in the second half.

In the locker room, Tiki urged the rest of the team to keep it up. "We've got to play the whole twenty minutes, not just fifteen or seventeen," he told them. "That team over there is too good. If we let up the least little bit, they'll sense it, and knock us flat."

"We're short one man," Rory pointed out. "I was running on empty there at the end, and we had a small forward playing out of position to fill in."

"Well, you've got to find your second wind," Tiki said flatly. "Don't worry, it's in there somewhere. Just keep telling yourself to *play proud*, and you'll find it."

Rory nodded, his jaw set with determination.

"We are not going down today!" Ronde said, and they all cheered as they headed out for the second half.

At the beginning of the game, the Rockets had been ambushed by the Eagles' energy. By now, though, they knew what they were up against. They would be confident in themselves, and why not? They were used to winning. They could always dial it up a notch when they had to, and they knew it.

Winning this game was going to take some doing, Tiki realized. He took a few pretend shots, without the ball, just to visualize it properly in his head. And then the whistle blew, and the second half began.

Rory Mathis started out on fire. He sank three straight shots, one of them a three-pointer, to give the Eagles a comfortable lead again. Tiki saw how Ronde would look for Rory, finding him with the pass at just the right moment—a second after he'd made his move, creating the space for the drive to the basket or the open jump shot.

Tiki had been right about the Rockets, too, though. Soon, they got their game together, and started swarming Ronde and Rory. Unlike Sugar, neither of them was very good at maintaining possession in the face of a double-team. They coughed up the ball four straight times, and finally, Coach Jackson had to call a time-out.

He put Tiki in for Ronde. Rory had to stay in the game, even though he was clearly flagging. Coach Jackson had been short by two players for this game, and he'd replaced them both with only one—Tiki. He might have fresh legs and wind, but he couldn't replace two tired guards at once!

The Rockets knew it. They eased up on Rory and focused all their pressure on Tiki. However, unlike Ronde, Tiki was used to keeping hold of the ball while under pressure. He stayed with his dribble now, and managed to find Rory open.

If Rory hadn't been so tired, he surely would have made the open shot. Instead, he left the ten-footer short. It barely even grazed the rim before hitting Bobby in the head and bouncing right to the Rockets' point guard. He raced right past the startled Eagle defenders, including Tiki, who was caught flat-footed. The kid laid the ball in, and suddenly, the Eagles' lead was all the way back down to one.

Tiki was determined to turn things around, but Rory needed a break, and Ronde was still getting his. Tiki slowed things down, playing catch with Bobby Dominic—in toward the basket, back out toward the point—until the clock wound down to five seconds. Then, passing it to Bobby one last time, he yelled, "Shoot!"

Bobby wasn't a bad athlete. He even had a bit of shooting touch. But he had never in his life been ordered to shoot. He stared at Tiki as he caught the ball, a look of utter confusion on his face.

"SHOOT!" Tiki screamed.

The buzzer went off with the ball still in Bobby's hands. Tiki wanted to react, to moan or throw his hands in the air. But he knew that would only discourage Bobby, and the Eagles needed all hands on deck. "Don't sweat it," he told Bobby instead as they backed up on defense. "Go for it next time."

Bobby nodded, his eyes regaining their focus. Next thing Tiki knew, Bobby had knocked the ball away from the Rockets' center. Tiki pounced on it, and a North Side player pounced on him. The whistle blew. "Foul!" yelled the referee.

Tiki went to the free-throw line with a one-on-one opportunity. If he sank the first shot, he got another. If he missed it . . . well, that was it.

He glanced at the sideline, and saw that Ronde was up and ready to come in between free throws. Tiki knew Rory was done. He was bent over, hands on his hips, staring at the floor. He'd been on the floor most of the first half, and hadn't had a break yet in the second. He'd been double-teamed the whole time.

Tiki knew he needed to sink this shot. He tossed it up. It clanged off the back of the rim. Tiki winced, and shouted, "No!" but it had no effect.

The Rockets dribbled back upcourt. Ronde remained

on the sideline. And Rory, gasping for breath, was way behind the play.

His man raced for the basket. The point guard threw an alley-oop. Rory's man grabbed it in mid-flight and laid it up and in. The Rockets had their first lead of the game!

By the time Ronde did manage to get back in the game, with ten minutes left to play, the Eagles were down by five.

Ronde was a great passer, but he needed Tiki to get free, and to sink his shots. Tiki knew the game depended on him now. If he could keep the Eagles close until Rory got his wind back, the Eagles would get a hugely needed boost.

Tiki regretted now that he'd ever bragged, to Ronde or anyone else, about his shooting prowess. It was one thing to sink a shot in your own driveway, or at the playground. It was another to sink one on the court against a first-place team, when *so much* was on the line.

He'd never been this nervous on the football field, and Tiki thought he knew why. His talents on the grid-iron were so strong that he'd always had a certain inner confidence. No matter what, deep down in his core, he knew he could force his will on the game, and turn the outcome his team's way most of the time.

He had no such confidence on the basketball court.

On the other hand, he did know how to be a team player. Right now, that meant getting free and sinking shots. Tiki forced all other thoughts—all doubts, all fears, all distractions—out of his head. He focused entirely on his man, on the ball, and on the basket.

The Rockets were swarming Ronde now. They obviously didn't fear Tiki, leaving him guarded by only one man. Tiki put a double-deke move on him, then held his hands up for the ball.

It was there, as soon as he turned to look. Ronde had timed the pass perfectly! Turning to the basket, Tiki put the ball up off the backboard, right in stride. Two points!

"Come on! Defense!" Tiki yelled as they jogged backward up the court. And now, the rest of the team seemed to rise to the moment. Larry Budnick blocked a shot, with Jake Lewis grabbing the rebound and outlet passing it to Ronde.

Tiki trailed his twin at a run. Ronde launched a no-look pass to him over his right shoulder. Tiki grabbed it, planted his feet, and let go a jumper. *Swish!*

Suddenly, there was an air of panic in the Rockets' home gym. The Rockets themselves seemed to share in the feeling. They were not used to being outplayed this late in a game. They launched two wild passes that resulted in turnovers.

Both times, Ronde managed to find the free man—

Larry once, and then Tiki again. When he put it through the hoop from long range, it gave the Eagles a four-point lead, with only six minutes left in the game.

There was a tension in the Rockets now, a wild look in their eyes. They seemed to stumble and lose their rhythm as a team. Tiki watched from the bench, out of breath, as a refreshed Rory reentered the fray, and proceeded to nail three straight jumpers.

The Rockets began fouling, a sure sign of desperation. And even though a lot of the Eagles missed their free throws, the Rockets couldn't convert on offense.

The Eagles defense was playing inspired ball. Everyone was helping everyone else whenever they needed it, and the mighty North Side Rockets just couldn't find a way to score.

In the end, the score was 71–58, Eagles. The team was back at .500, with one game left to play. They'd beaten the runaway league leaders convincingly, without their superstar! They could go forward with confidence now into their final game.

Except for one thing, thought Tiki. In that final game, he would not be on the team. Dave Bassin would be back from his injury, presumably. And Sugar's suspension would be over. There would be no room for Tiki on the team he'd just helped lead to victory—and everyone in the visiting locker room knew it.

One by one, they all came up to Tiki and shook his

hand and hugged him. "Thanks," they all said. "You played awesome ball."

Tiki felt good that he'd played so well. Best of all was that he and Ronde together had led the team to this important victory.

Ronde would be back at substitute shooting guard for the final game. And Tiki would be back at Landzberg's, shuffling boxes between shelves.

He and Ronde exchanged their personal handshake and hugged each other. "That goes on our lifetime highlight reel, yo," said Ronde with a wide grin.

"Yeah," said Tiki, his feelings in turmoil.

"You were fantastic, Tiki. I've got to give it up to you. You said you could shoot, and you proved it. No doubt."

"You got me the ball at the right time," said Tiki modestly.

"I did, didn't I?" Ronde agreed with a big smile. "But you put the ball in the net. I could not have done that."

"Well, you'd better practice between now and next game," Tiki pointed out.

"Why? You think Sugar's gonna get me the ball? Come on."

Tiki shrugged. "I don't know. Maybe he read my column and will change his mind."

"Yeah," said Ronde with a sad laugh. "And maybe I'll find a hundred-dollar bill in the street."

• • •

Funny, thought Tiki afterward, *how life turns out. Just when you think there's no way around an obstacle, something surprising happens, and there is the way, staring you in the face.*

He was late getting to the team bus—last one out of the locker room. As he crossed the empty North Side gym, he heard a familiar voice call out to him. "Barber!"

He stopped, looking up at the bleachers. There was Sugar Morton, coming down the rows toward him! He walked straight up to Tiki, looking right at him.

"What are you doing here?" Tiki asked.

"It's a free country, isn't it?" Sugar retorted. "I rode over on my bike."

"That's what, three miles?" Tiki tried to guess. "Weren't you freezing?"

Sugar shrugged. "I wasn't going to miss this game." He had a bitter look on his face. "No matter what anybody says, I *do* care about this team."

"I know you do," Tiki said. "Um, listen, they're all waiting for me on the bus. . . ."

"Yeah, anyway, what I wanted to say . . . I saw the whole game. You and Ronde did a great job running the team."

"Huh?" Tiki was stunned. It was the last thing he'd expected Sugar to say.

"You got the whole team playing great. And they beat a great squad on their home court. When I get back, I'm going to run the team just like you guys did . . . spread the ball around more. You really showed me something, man."

Tiki nodded soberly. "Well, that's good, Sugar. I . . . I guess you read my column, then?"

"I read it," Sugar admitted. "And I get what you were saying. But it's the way you *played* today that showed me you were right about everything. I can't be treating the team like it's their fault my family's a mess. After all, they're my family too, in a way. Right?"

"Hey," said Tiki. "Your family's going to work it out, one way or another. Just hang in there . . . and remember, your mother loves you too—no matter what she thought she had to do. Give her a chance to make it up to you, and you'll see."

Sugar was silent, staring at the floor. "Don't you have a bus to catch?" he finally replied.

Tiki left him there, in the darkened gym, a lonely figure, but one who'd learned at least one key lesson. Tiki only hoped it would help him heal as much as it would help the Eagles win.

He sat quietly on the bus while the other team members whooped it up, celebrating the biggest win of their season.

On the one hand, he was pleased that Sugar seemed to be getting the message. On the other hand, he'd really enjoyed his moment in the sun on the basketball court.

In the end, though, he decided he was satisfied. After all, there was no doubt Sugar was a better basketball player than he was. Besides, in addition to helping the Eagles win this one key game, Tiki had done an even more important service for the team—he'd taught them to *play* like one.

13

A TEAM CALLED THE EAGLES

Ronde couldn't help but feel a little letdown at the team's next practice. Instead of Tiki's intensity and excitement, there was Sugar, back again and in control. Dave Bassin was also there, his eye back to normal, thank goodness. But that meant there was no room anymore for Tiki.

Ronde could tell he wasn't the only one who was disappointed. The team had played its best overall game of the year without Sugar. Would its members respond to his leadership, now that they'd had a taste of life without him at the helm?

Ronde realized, of course, that Tiki couldn't have kept it up anyway. Mr. Landzberg had not been happy about giving him the day off for the last game. Letting him take two more days—for practice and the team's final game—was out of the question.

And Ronde sure wasn't about to give up his *own* spot on the team to cover Tiki. With Sugar back at point guard, Ronde was more valuable for his defense than Tiki would have been for his shooting.

What really hurt was that Tiki would not even get to be there for the big game against the Panthers of Jefferson Junior High. With their school located just half a mile from Hidden Valley, the Panthers were the Eagles' arch-rivals in every sport (except football, where they'd never been much of a factor). Jefferson had a winning record, but the Panthers would only make the play-offs if they beat the Eagles.

If having a shot at a winning season wasn't enough to motivate our team, thought Ronde, spoiling the Panthers' chances ought to give the players added juice.

This was going to be an exciting game, even if Sugar tried to do it all by himself. Ronde wished Tiki could have been there, but he understood. The money from his job was important to their family right now, and that had to come first.

Ronde was worried about these Eagles, though. Looking around, he saw Rory and Bobby hanging their heads. Larry looked distracted, and Jake seemed downright bored.

None of them wanted to play with Sugar at the point, Ronde realized. He had been their superstar, the one they all looked up to—but with his selfish behavior, his pouting, his sniping and raging at his teammates, he'd lost their trust.

But if Ronde was worried, that was because he'd assumed he was looking at the *same Sugar Morton*. And *that*, it turned out, was a *mistake*.

As soon as Dave Bassin came into the gym, he got a round of applause from his teammates—including Sugar. Then, as if that wasn't enough, Sugar came up to him and offered his hand.

Dave didn't shake it right away, but Ronde saw Sugar lean in toward him, saying something Ronde could only imagine was an apology. Sugar seemed to look closely at Dave's eye, wincing at the bruise that was still plain to see.

Finally, Dave nodded, and the two boys shook hands. Looking around, Ronde saw the surprise on everyone's faces. Even Coach Jackson seemed unprepared for this unlikely turn of events.

Ronde shook his head. Coach J. had done little to correct what was wrong with his team. He'd gone and recruited Ronde and Tiki, and more or less left it up to them to transform Sugar's attitude.

However, from the looks of what he was seeing now, the coach's strategy seemed to have worked! Sugar began leading drills—three men running downcourt—

one in the middle, one on either side, passing back and forth, the ball never touching the ground, until one of them tossed up a layup.

Usually, Sugar would insist on being the one taking the shot. Today, though, he made sure he dished off to one of the kids running alongside him, every time.

When they did sprints, Sugar, who always won, or became upset if he didn't, eased up so that Dave Bassin could reach the finish line first.

Ronde exchanged wary glances with Bobby and Rory. They were obviously as surprised as he was that Sugar seemed so much more humble and giving.

Of course, this was just *practice*. Ronde was not yet convinced that, come game time, Sugar wouldn't revert to his usual ball-hogging ways. Still, for now at least, it was a refreshing change.

Then, before the scrimmage, Sugar actually asked Coach Jackson for permission to speak to his teammates. Coach J., stunned, shrugged and said, "Sure, Sugar. Go ahead."

"Okay," Sugar said, when he was sure they were all paying attention. "I just want to say that I know I've been a jerk sometimes." He drew in a deep breath, then blew it out. The rest of the team was dead silent.

"I've been having some . . . well, some problems . . . at home . . . and . . ." He paused, gathered himself, and continued: "I know I took some of my temper out on a lot of you guys . . . and that hurt the team. So I want to say, I'm sorry for that, and . . . it won't happen again."

He bit his lip and blinked his eyes several times in rapid succession. "I hope you'll all forgive me, and that we can play like a team this week against Jefferson. I'm sure going to do everything I can to make it that way, starting right now."

He clenched his jaw, looked over at Coach Jackson, and nodded. "I guess that's it," he finished.

Coach J. smiled, nodded back, and clapped Sugar on the shoulder. "You're a good man, Morton," he said. "Okay, boys—let's give it a go!"

Everyone burst into a spontaneous cheer, whistling, clapping and shouting, "Yeah!"

Now it was back to practice, and the mood in the gym could not have been more different from how it was before. Everyone had a bounce in his step, a gleam in his eye, and a smile on his face.

Sugar was everywhere, dishing the ball, spreading it around, shouting encouragement to his teammates, and generally being the leader they'd wanted him to be all along. Ronde could scarcely believe the change in him—but he certainly welcomed it!

When practice was over, he waited around for most of the others to leave. Then he approached Sugar. "Unbelievable," he said, smiling and shaking his head. "What happened to you, dude?"

Sugar furrowed his brow. "What are you talking about, Barber?"

"Come on! You know!" Ronde said with a laugh. "Are you Sugar's identical twin, or what?"

Sugar had to laugh. "Okay, okay," he said. "I'm just messing with you."

"So what really happened?" Ronde pressed him.

"Oh, I don't know," said Sugar. "I read your brother's column, for one thing."

"I told you it'd be worth your while."

"But that wasn't really it," Sugar stopped him. "It was more the way you two guys ran the team that last game. I watched the whole thing—did Tiki tell you?"

Ronde did recall Tiki mentioning something about Sugar being there, but the brothers hadn't really had time to talk about it.

"I thought about what you said too," Sugar went on. "That night when you came to my house?" Sugar clapped him on the shoulder. "Thanks for hanging in there with me. I don't think I would have gotten through this without a little help from my friends. And by friends, I mean you and Tiki."

"Well, gee," Ronde said, a little embarrassed by the compliment, "we were just trying to help—" He'd been about to say "the team," but didn't want Sugar to think they didn't care about him personally.

"And you did," Sugar said. "I actually took some of

your advice, too—about *other* things, I mean."

Ronde was dying to know what Sugar meant, but he figured that if Sugar wanted him to know the details, he would have shared them. So he left it at that. Instead, he simply offered Sugar his hand, and the two boys shook on it.

"Great," Sugar said. "Now let's go beat the Panthers!"

"I hear that!" Ronde agreed. "Let's make this a winning season!"

Ronde could feel the familiar game-day rush of adrenaline as he suited up for the Eagles' final game. This was why he'd been excited to be a player again, even if it was on a basketball court instead of a football field.

Today, there was a lot of added pressure. This was a big game, for sure. Also, since the Eagles weren't going to make the play-offs either way, it was definitely their last game of the season.

If they won, it would mean so much—to everyone on the team, to the Hidden Valley fans, who'd expected so much of their team this year, only to be disappointed. And most of all, to Sugar.

During these past few weeks, Sugar's life at home had been in crisis. Ronde wondered how *he* would have handled things if he were in Sugar's place. After all, it was easy to see what other people were doing wrong in their lives. Seeing your *own* faults was much harder.

And Sugar had certainly grown a lot since Tiki and Ronde had joined the team.

If they won today, Sugar could take that precious feeling with him into the future. He could work on his own happiness, on his leadership and basketball skills, so that when he came back next fall as a ninth grader, he would lead a more experienced team than before—and would lead it better.

On the other hand, if the Eagles lost today, it might just prove to Sugar that all the changes he'd made in his attitude were a waste of time. He might go right back to dumping his anger on everyone around him, just like before.

So yes, this game might be important to a lot of people, Ronde included—but it was *everything* to Sugar Morton.

Ronde looked over at him, standing on the other side of the court, casually shooting (and sinking) shot after shot in pregame warmups.

Sugar had an ease about him that Ronde hadn't noticed before. Was Sugar really that calm? Or was it just a good job of masking the energy inside him?

It didn't take long to find out. Right off the opening tip, Sugar was everywhere on the court. He stole the ball from the opposing point guard, and quickly tossed it inside to Bobby Dominic, who was ridiculously free, since all the Panthers had immediately swarmed Sugar.

So free was Bobby, in fact, that he held the ball for an instant, not sure what to do with it. All season, he'd have felt pressured to pass it back to Sugar. But now, Sugar was yelling at him, "SHOOT! SHOOT!"

Bobby did, and the ball caromed off the backboard and in. It was a good start for the Eagles, and the grin on Bobby's face was soon shared by all the members of the team.

The Eagles laid a suffocating defense on the Panthers, forcing turnovers and bad shots, while on offense, Sugar was beating the double-team by making quick passes to the men left free by the defenders.

Rory, Bobby, Larry, and Jake didn't make all their shots, but that was understandable. They weren't used to shooting when Sugar was on the court.

Soon it was Ronde's turn to enter the game off the bench. Only a so-so shooter at the best of times, Ronde wasn't looking to score—just to get rebounds, play good defense, and maybe help out on the fast break.

But Sugar kept finding him free on the perimeter, and Ronde found himself with open shots.

With Sugar's call of "SHOOT!" ringing in his ears, Ronde launched a couple of shots he had no prayer of making—and was amazed to see them both go in!

The first ten minutes of the game were amazing, with the Eagles playing their best basketball of the season. The Panthers seemed panicked, off-balance—

but Ronde knew they weren't done yet. Not by a long shot. The Panthers were a good team, and they needed this game to make the play-offs. That made them a desperate bunch.

When Coach J. subbed Dave Bassin for Sugar, the Panthers saw their chance. They swarmed Dave over and over again, forcing turnovers and cutting the gap to a mere seven points before Sugar came back in with five minutes left in the half.

Their star might have returned, but the rest of the Eagles were tired. They'd been playing with such high energy that they were bound to flag sooner or later, while the Panthers, with a much deeper bench, kept coming at them with pressure defense and a running style of play that left the Eagles breathless.

Only Ronde seemed to have the stamina to keep up the pace. His conditioning as a cornerback, running sprints down the field over and over again, gave him better endurance than most kids his age.

But even Ronde was starting to tire by the end of the first half. The score, 32–29, was still in their favor—but for how long? Was the Eagles' burst of energy played out? Or did they have another half of great basketball left in them?

Sugar was silent in the locker room, but everyone else was excited, even if they were exhausted by the effort they'd just given. They all high-fived Sugar, and one another, knowing that they'd lifted their game to a higher level as a team.

But Ronde—and Sugar—knew that was not going to be enough by itself to beat the Panthers today. Their opponents were bigger, stronger, and overall, faster, not to mention deeper.

If the Eagles were going to beat them, it would have to be on the strength of their desire. They would have to have the hearts and souls of hardcourt warriors.

Ronde wished that Tiki were there in the locker room with them. With both of them revving up the team, he knew these Eagles would find the inner strength to win.

But on his own, tired as he was, he was afraid that he just couldn't manage it. He was still breathing too hard to talk, and his heart was pounding so loudly he was sure everyone could hear it.

By the time he'd recovered enough to consider saying something to psych up the rest of the team, it was too late. Coach was already ushering them back into the gym, where the bleachers full of screaming Eagle fans were yelling so loudly Ronde couldn't even hear himself think!

Coach Jackson pointed to him, indicating that Ronde was going to start the half at shooting guard. He high-fived Rory, who was still panting heavily, and went out to join Sugar and the rest of the team.

This time, as before, the tip-off went to the Panthers.

But this time, they were clearly trying a different tactic. Instead of rushing the ball upcourt, they went slow and steady, with the point guard dribbling in place for several seconds, surveying the battlefield as his teammates made their moves. Finally, he found the center free for a long pass and a quick layup.

On defense, the Panthers kept up their fierce pressure. Sugar was able to avoid it the first few times, but now the defenders were anticipating him passing off. They faked double-teams, only to back off when Sugar had stopped dribbling.

Suddenly, it was hard for the rest of the Eagles to get free. Sugar wound up taking a flat-footed shot that clanged off the rim, short.

Over the next few minutes, the lead seesawed back and forth. All the Eagles' points were on awkward shots by Sugar, who, despite not being able to shoot in rhythm, was managing to sink half his attempts.

The rest of the Eagles were exhausting themselves on defense, trying to keep up with the many passes the Panthers were making, spreading the defense thin and tiring them out.

Soon, the Eagles were getting themselves into serious foul trouble. Bobby Dominic had to sit down, and so did Ronde.

Then, Coach J. gave Sugar a rest too. It was like a smoke signal to the Panthers, who proceeded to reignite their running game. Without Sugar and Ronde on the court, the Eagles soon found themselves behind by five, and fading fast.

Sugar wanted to get back into the game as much as Ronde did. But he was so out of breath he couldn't even manage to ask the coach to put him back out there.

Ronde began to have a terrible, sinking feeling. After all the progress they'd made, were these Eagles about to lose this final, most important game of the year?

By the time Sugar got back in there, they might be too far behind to catch up!

Ronde bit his lip, worried. If only something could flip that energy switch back on—the energy that had lit up the Eagles at the start of the game. . . .

That's when Ronde saw the doors at the far end of the gym open and two new spectators enter the room.

Ronde stood up and waved excitedly. "Tiki!" he yelled. In spite of the noise in the gym, Tiki spotted his twin and waved back, grinning broadly before finding a seat in the bleachers.

That's when Ronde noticed who the other new arrival was—*Sugar's mom*.

Ronde turned to look at Sugar, and was surprised to see a tear trickling down his cheek. Sugar hurriedly wiped it away, hoping no one had seen it—but when his mom waved to him, smiling hopefully, Sugar waved back.

That made Ronde smile inside. As important as it was for him to see Tiki walking in, what must it have meant to Sugar to have his mom show up, after all they'd been through?

Coach Jackson tapped Ronde on the shoulder. "You're back in," he said. "Sugar, you ready too?"

Sugar's eyes were on fire. "You bet!" he said. "Come on, Barber, let's show these clowns who's boss!"

They high-fived each other as they jogged back onto the court. The score was 45–40, Jefferson, with eight minutes left to play.

Plenty of time, Ronde told himself, suddenly confident deep inside. He had a feeling this was going to be ten minutes of action he would never forget.

No sooner did play resume than Sugar went on a tear, streaking down the court with the ball, putting on impossible moves, sinking shots, making no-look passes, stealing balls, rebounding, and generally taking over the game.

In all of that, though, he never forgot that there were four other Eagles on the floor. In the scoring blitz that followed, every one of them had at least four points.

The Panthers were in chaos at first, but once their lead had disappeared, they seemed to find a way to stay even with the Eagles. Ronde could see that this one was going to come down to the wire—but he never doubted that the Eagles would end up on top.

Behind by only a few points, the Panthers struggled furiously to win the game. They couldn't stop Sugar, so they began to foul him, hard. He cried out in pain a couple times—but he sank every one of his free throws.

When the Panthers saw that their strategy was backfiring, they came at the other Eagles instead. They would foul Ronde or one of the others in a one-and-one situation. If the first free throw was missed, there was no second shot, so the Panthers would get the ball back, and could catch up.

But this strategy didn't work either. No matter how inaccurate their normal shooting touch was, on this occasion—at this critical moment—*every* member of the Eagles sank *every* free throw he took. One . . . and one . . . and *another* . . . and *another* . . .

With only two minutes left in the game, the Panthers' point guard hit a three-pointer to bring Jefferson within one big shot of tying the game. Now they stopped fouling, just playing tight defense instead—not overreacting to Sugar's moves, but not letting him penetrate to the basket either.

Sugar made a perfectly good pass to Larry Budnick, but one of the Panthers saw it coming, made the steal, and raced the other way. Ahead of everyone, he could have pulled up and tried for a game-tying three-pointer. But he went for the easy layup instead, figuring a sure two points was better. There was still enough time for another possession—if the Panthers could get a stop.

It had all come down to this last minute, Ronde thought. Could the Eagles stave off the Panthers' furious comeback?

Sugar went slowly, walking the ball down the court, letting the precious seconds tick down. He must have known the Panthers would panic and come after him sooner or later. And they did.

With only twenty seconds on the clock, he faked a drive, then dished off to Ronde at the point.

Afterward, Ronde was never sure whether or not he actually heard Sugar yell "SHOOT!" But whether the voice was in his head or for real, Ronde didn't think twice. He heard "SHOOT!" and he *shot*.

SWISH!

The roar of the crowd as they leaped to their feet echoed off the gym walls as Ronde threw his hands over his head in triumph.

But the ref quickly signaled that it was only a two-pointer, because Ronde's foot had been on the line.

"Dang!" Ronde moaned. That meant the Panthers would have one more shot at it, with fifteen seconds to play after their time-out.

Coach J. huddled the Eagles together. "We've really played like a team today," he told them. "And we're gonna win this game if we keep it up for fifteen more seconds! Now get out there and WIN!!!"

Ronde had never heard or seen the coach sound so excited. He'd never really stopped to consider what this all must mean to Coach J. But it felt good to know that he and Tiki had been a part of changing this team for the better.

The Eagles went back out there. One more defensive stop, and they would go down in the record books as a winning team.

The Panthers inbounded, and their point guard, pressured by Sugar, passed it to Ronde's man.

There were only ten seconds left as Ronde tracked his man's dribble. He knew the kid had to be nervous— so he faked a sudden grab at the ball.

Sure enough, it threw the kid off, just enough to lose control of his dribble slightly. By the time he'd recovered, Sugar was there too, on the double-team. The panicked Jefferson player threw it up for grabs, hoping that one of his teammates would come up with it. . . .

But it was Bobby D. who held the ball when the buzzer sounded! Eagles 82, Panthers 80!

The crowd erupted, flowing out of the bleachers like lava. The whole place was shaking from their feet pounding on the floor.

Tiki ran up to Ronde and hugged him, both of them jumping up and down.

For Ronde, at that moment, life was every bit as beautiful as when the twins had won the state championship in football. Even though this was only a game that brought the team above .500 for the season, and these Eagles would not be going to the play-offs, it didn't matter. What mattered was that they'd done what they came to do—they'd helped straighten out a team that was a mess before they got there, and turn it into a winner.

Next year, with Sugar in ninth grade, and all the rest of its starters returning, these Eagles would surely contend for a play-off spot, maybe even the league championship.

Ronde wanted to tell Tiki how much it meant to him to look up and see him there in the stands. Tiki had arrived at the key moment, and him being there had given Ronde the strength to overcome his exhaustion, both mental and physical.

He wanted to tell Tiki that, but he didn't. It was hard to say things like that, even to your twin brother. Besides, it was noisy as all get-out in that gym.

So Ronde simply said, "How'd you get here?"

"Ralphie covered for me," Tiki said with a big grin.

"His aunt took care of his mom?"

"Even better!" said Tiki. "His mom's doing much better."

"Really? That's fantastic!"

"Yeah, the money she got from Mr. Landzberg helped her get a new kind of treatment. She said Ralphie could go back to work full-time from now on!"

"Wow!" Ronde was blown away. There must have been a whole lot of money in those envelopes he and Tiki had delivered. *Another important mission,* he thought.

Mr. Landzberg and the people who worked for him were like another kind of family, really. Just like this basketball team was a kind of family.

But Ronde knew there was no kind of family as precious as your *real* family. He looked over to the far side of the gym, and saw Sugar and his mom hugging each other. It felt really good to Ronde to know he'd been part of that, as well.

"Come on, Tiki," he said. "Let's get out of here. I want to take you over to Kessler's and get you your favorite ice-cream sundae—on me!"

"What?" Tiki said, pretending to faint. *"You,* pay for *me*? Excuse me, would you give me a pinch on the arm. I must be dreaming!"

"Come on, man, cut me some slack. I've been saving every penny for Mom," Ronde said.

"Oh! I almost forgot to tell you!" Tiki gasped. "Mom got a raise—and a bonus, too!"

"She *did*?"

"Yeah—I saw her after school on my way to Landzberg's, and she was all excited. She said we didn't need to hand over our paychecks anymore!"

"Cool!" Ronde said. "In that case, I'll buy you *two* ice-cream sundaes!"

"You know what I was thinking, though?" Tiki said as they exited the building and headed down the street toward Kessler's Ice Cream Parlor. "Baseball tryouts are next week. And they've got *lots* of openings. . . ."

"You mean . . . ?"

"What do you think? I think we'd look good out on the field together."

"Word!" Ronde agreed. "But I'm playing center field."

"No way. You play left or right. I'm a better outfielder than you."

"Get out! I'm faster than you!"

"But I get a better jump on the ball."

"I've got softer hands."

"I'm a better hitter. . . ."

And so it went on as they entered Kessler's, ordered, and wolfed down their sundaes.

One season might be over, but another one was just beginning. And Tiki and Ronde would always be up for the challenge.

BASKETBALL MOVES

Cut: An offensive move where a player who is not holding the ball quickly changes their position on the court to a better spot. This may be done to receive a pass from a player or to help defend a teammate.

Double-team: In this defensive strategy, a coach puts two defenders on one offensive player to keep the opponent from making a shot. However, this takes a defender away from another teammate who can make the shot while no one is blocking him or her.

Dribble drive motion: Players on a team place themselves near the layup and three-pointer lines with the shooter in the center, in this play. Similar to isolation, this allows the shooter to go one-on-one with the defender and dribble toward the basket. If another defender comes in to help block, however, the shooter passes to the open teammate, who makes a layup or three-point shot.

Fast break: The defender for a team blocks their opponent's shot and quickly takes the ball in this offensive play. The defender then runs to the opposite side of the court and quickly shoots the ball before the opponent can set up defenses.

Hook Shot: In this move a shooter holds the ball in one hand and makes an arc over his or her head as he or she shoots the ball into the basket. This type of shot is difficult for players to block.

Isolation: In an isolation play, teammates of the player holding the ball move to the side of the court, taking their defenders with them. This allows the shooter to go one-on-one with their defender, with less chances of double-teaming.

Pass-and-cut: In this offensive play the player holding the ball passes to a teammate and quickly runs—cuts—toward the basket. When the player gets close to the basket, a teammate passes the ball back to shoot.

Pick-and-roll: In this offensive play, either a forward or center player screens the defender of a teammate, the shooting guard. The forward or center then turns to receive a pass from the shooting guard, and shoots the ball.

Pump fake: This is a trick move. The player who is holding the ball acts as if he or she is going to shoot or pass the ball, but keeps it instead. Players do this in order to get their defender to leave from a spot, while they go in another direction.

Screen: Also known as a pick. The screen is a defensive move where a player blocks an opponent, keeping him or her from moving to a better place on the basketball court. Players do this to help a teammate shoot, pass, or run toward the basket.

Tomahawk dunk: For this dunk a player takes the ball with both hands, puts it behind his or her neck while in midair, and slams the ball into the hoop to make the shot.

Triangle offense: This offensive play was popular with the Chicago Bulls and Los Angeles Lakers. In this, teammates place themselves into a triangle on the court that is wide enough to stop double-teaming, yet close enough to pass to teammates without an interception.